KU-483-347

The Secret Circle

THE DIVIDE

Created by
L.J. SMITH

Written by Aubrey Clark

Hodder
Children's
Books

A division of Hachette Children's Books

A Catalogue record for this book is available from the British Library

ISBN: 978 1 444 91269 2

Typeset in Futura by Avon DataSet Ltd,
Bidford on Avon, Warwickshire

Printed in Great Britain by
Clays Ltd, St Ives plc

The paper and board used in this paperback by Hodder Children's Books
are natural recyclable products made from wood grown in
sustainable forests. The manufacturing processes conform to the
environmental regulations of the country of origin.

Hodder Children's Books
a division of Hachette Children's Books
338 Euston Road, London NW1 3BH
An Hachette Livre UK Company
www.hachette.co.uk

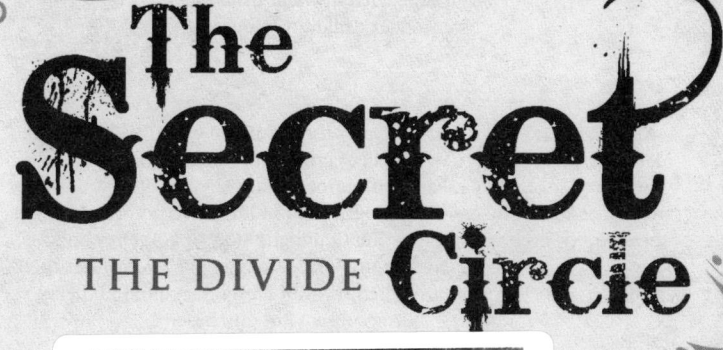

The Secret

THE DIVIDE   Circle

Chapter One

Adam's car windows were foggy with the heat of their breath. It was a balmy night at dusk and the air was scented with early signs of spring – a perfect night to roll down the windows and enjoy the breeze while they kissed. But Cassie insisted the windows stay closed, for privacy. Besides, she liked the feeling of being cocooned in such close quarters with Adam, insulated from the outside world by the steamy glass. They were going to be late for their meeting, but inside this cloud, she didn't care.

'We should go in,' she said half-heartedly.

'Just five more minutes. It's not like they can start without you.'

Right, Cassie thought, *because I'm a leader. All the more reason not to be late because I'm making out with my boyfriend.*

Boyfriend. The notion still made her giddy, even after all these weeks. She watched the way the setting sun brought out the multicoloured highlights in Adam's tangled hair – shades of burgundy and orange – and the crystalline sparkle in his blue eyes.

He leaned in and softly kissed that spot on the side of Cassie's neck just below her ear. 'Fine,' she said. 'Three more minutes.'

Their first kiss as a couple had changed everything for Cassie. It meant something. Adam's lips on hers felt deliberate and momentous, like an agreement, and Cassie's whole body became aware of that fact. This was love, she'd realised.

Cassie assumed the sensation would lessen as the days passed, that their kissing would become routine and habitual, but it hadn't. If anything, its intensity increased over time. Parked now just outside the old lighthouse on Shore Road, Cassie knew they had to stop kissing, but she couldn't. And neither could Adam. The quickening of his breath and the pressing urgency of his grip on her hips made that obvious.

But it wouldn't look good to walk in late to her first meeting as a Circle leader. 'We really have to go in,' she said, pulling away and placing her hand up against

Adam's chest to hold him still.

He took a deep breath and exhaled through his mouth, trying to cool himself down. 'I know.'

Reluctantly, he let Cassie disentangle from his embrace and make herself more presentable. After a few more deep breaths and a swift patting down of his wild hair, he followed her inside.

Walking across the long-grassed meadow that led to the old lighthouse, Cassie couldn't help but be struck by its worn, rustic beauty. Melanie had told them it dated back to the late 1700s, and its age was evident in its dilapidated appearance. The tower itself was constructed of greyed stone and brick reaching almost ninety feet high, but at its base was a small, crumbling wooden house – the light-keeper's cottage. It had been built for the lightkeeper's wife and children, so they could be close to him while he saw to his duties upstairs. According to Melanie, the cottage was passed down through several generations until the lighthouse was finally decommissioned in the early 1900s. Since then, there had been talk of converting it into a museum, but it had remained abandoned for decades.

Adam smiled at her, and her breath caught in her throat. She unlatched the cottage door and stepped inside,

3

Adam just behind her. With an almost audible *whoosh*, the Circle's focus shifted to her grand, belated entrance.

It was immediately obvious that they'd kept the group waiting for too long, and that the group knew exactly what she and Adam had been doing. Cassie examined all their faces, absorbing their different reactions and silent accusations.

Melanie's usually cool eyes contained a heated impatience, and Laurel shyly giggled. Deborah, sitting on the edge of the wooden bench in the corner, appeared ready to make a snide comment, but before she had the chance, Chris and Doug Henderson, who'd been playing catch with a tennis ball by the window, said in unison, 'Well, it's about frigging time.'

Nick, sitting on the floor with his back against the wall, looked at Cassie with a subtle pain in his eyes that forced her to turn away.

'Adam,' Faye said in her lazy, husky voice, 'your lip gloss is smudged.'

The room broke out with uncontrollable laughter, and Adam's face reddened. Diana stared straight down at the floor, humiliated for them, or perhaps for herself. She'd been gracious about Adam being with Cassie now, but there was only so much a girl could take.

4

'We call this meeting to order,' Diana said, regaining her poise. 'Everyone, please be seated.'

Diana spoke as if the laughter had died down, but it was still loud and raucous. 'The first order of business,' she continued, 'is what we're going to do with the Master Tools.'

That quieted the group. The Master Tools – the diadem, the silver bracelet, and the leather garter – had belonged to Black John's original coven. They'd been hidden for hundreds of years until Cassie figured out they were concealed within the fireplace in her grandmother's kitchen. The Circle had used the Tools to defeat Black John, but they'd put off making any decisions regarding them since. Tonight, the time had come to determine their fate.

'That's right,' Cassie said, joining Diana in the centre of the room. 'We have real power now. And we need to . . .'

What? What did they need to do? Cassie turned to Diana. Her green eyes and shining hair were radiant, even in the ghostly lantern light of the old cottage. If anyone knew what the Circle should do next, it was Diana.

'I think we should destroy the power of the Master Tools somehow,' Diana said in her clear, musical voice. 'So no one can use them.'

For a moment, nobody spoke. They were all too shocked by this suggestion. Then Faye broke the silence. 'You've got to be kidding me,' she said. 'You and Adam have spent half your lives trying to find the Master Tools.'

'I know,' Diana said. 'But after all we've been through, and now that we've defeated Black John, I feel like that much power can't be good for us, or for anyone.'

Cassie was as surprised as Faye. These words didn't sound like Diana at all, or at least not like the Diana that Cassie had known.

Adam appeared taken aback as well, but he kept quiet. Leaders spoke first. Those were the rules.

Cassie felt the attention of the group settle upon her. They were a triumvirate now, which meant her power was equal to both Diana's and Faye's. She wanted to use her authority well, to state her opinion openly and intelligently, but she didn't want to go against Diana.

'What made you change your mind?' she said.

Diana crossed her thin arms over her chest. 'People change their minds all the time, Cassie.'

'Well,' Faye said, focusing on Diana with her honey-coloured eyes, 'I disagree entirely. It would be a waste to not use the Tools. At the very least, we should experiment with them.' Her mouth formed a cruel smile. 'Don't you agree, Cassie?'

'Um,' she said. It was weird. Cassie kind of agreed with Faye on this one, which may have been the first time she ever agreed with Faye on anything. She didn't want to side with Faye over Diana, but how could they just destroy the Tools? What if Black John came back? These were their only means of self-defence. She wished Diana had discussed this with her before now.

'We can talk to Constance for help getting rid of them,' Diana offered. 'If that's what we decide to do.'

Melanie's great-aunt Constance had been helping the Circle with their magic. Since she'd tapped into her powers to nurse Cassie's mother back to health last winter, she'd become more willing to share her knowledge of the old ways.

'Constance probably knows a spell we can use,' Diana said. 'And with Black John gone for good, I bet she'll agree it's time to put the Tools to rest.'

Cassie could see Diana felt strongly about this. As did Faye – that familiar fiery anger had snuck its way into her sharp features.

'We should take a vote,' a strong voice called out. It belonged to Nick, who rarely spoke at Circle meetings.

Hearing him express an opinion on this caught Cassie off guard.

'Nick's right,' Melanie said. 'We should all have equal say in a decision so important.'

Diana nodded. 'I'm fine with that.'

Faye dramatically swept her red nails at the group. 'Vote then,' she said, with the confidence of someone who'd already won.

Melanie stood and stepped to the centre of the room. She always called out Circle votes, Cassie noticed. 'All those in favour of destroying the Master Tools,' she said, 'raise your hands.'

Diana's hand went up first, followed by Melanie's own, then Laurel's. After a second-long pause, Nick raised his, and then finally Adam.

Cassie couldn't believe it. Adam had voted with Diana, even though she knew he'd rather experiment with the Tools.

'All those in favour of keeping the Tools,' Melanie said, 'raise your—'

'Wait,' Cassie called out. She'd gotten distracted and lost the chance to choose Diana's side.

Faye laughed. 'You snooze, you lose, Cassie. And a vote against Diana is a vote for me.'

'Wrong,' Cassie said, surprising herself as she said it. 'It's a vote for me.'

She paused to look at Adam and saw he was smiling proudly.

'I propose a third option,' she said. 'We keep the Tools, in case we need them. We don't destroy their power, but we also don't experiment with them.'

'In that case,' Faye said, 'I'd be happy to keep the Tools safe until we need them.'

'Not a chance,' Adam said.

Cassie raised her hand. 'I wasn't finished.' She eyed Faye and then Diana. 'I propose that each leader hide one of the three relics, so they can only be used if the whole group knows about it.'

Everyone got quiet then, as they mulled over this new possibility in their minds.

It was a good idea, and Cassie knew it. What she didn't know was how she'd come up with it right there on the spot like that. When she took control of the floor, she hadn't had the slightest idea what she was going to say.

Diana spoke first. 'That does seem like a fair compromise,' she said. 'Melanie, I call for a revote.'

'I second the call for a revote,' Nick said gallantly.

Melanie raised her eyebrows. 'Okay then. All those in favour of . . . Cassie's idea, raise your hands.'

All hands went up, except for Deborah's, Suzan's and Faye's.

'It's decided then,' Melanie said.

Faye stood perfectly still. She didn't move a muscle, but a dark shadow fell over her face.

Suzan bounced out of her chair. 'Oh, well,' she said. 'I guess that's that. I'm starving. Can we go eat now?'

'Yeah, let's go get tacos,' Sean said.

One by one, everyone stood up and began gathering their things, talking about meeting at Melanie's great-aunt Constance's later to practise their invocations. Diana snuffed out the candles and turned down the lanterns. All the while, Faye remained motionless.

'You,' she said.

Instinctively, Cassie took a step back even though Faye was across the room.

'Don't be too proud of yourself.' She sauntered over to Cassie and leaned in close. Cassie could smell her heady perfume and it made her dizzy. 'You may have won the battle,' Faye said. 'But . . . well, you know.'

Cassie drew away from Faye's reach. Her fear still got the best of her every time Faye threatened her. Whether or not Faye was actually stronger was beside the point. She had the singleness of mind of a sociopath and a complete lack of conscience. Faye couldn't be reasoned with, and that was what made her dangerous.

'We're on the same side,' Cassie said weakly. 'We want the same thing.'

Faye narrowed her honey-coloured eyes. 'Not really,' she said. 'Not yet, anyway.'

It sounded like a threat, and Cassie knew Faye never made an empty threat.

Chapter Two

Cassie and Adam barely said a word the whole drive back to Cassie's house. She was still shaken up by Faye's words, and Adam, sensing that, just quietly held her hand while he drove.

She clicked on the radio for a pleasant distraction and fiddled with its dial till she found a song she liked. She couldn't remember the song's title, but it triggered a feeling of nostalgia in her heart, a memory of a time when her life was much simpler than it was now. She had been in New Salem less than a year, but it felt like forever and a day.

Instead of watching the spring night drift by her window, Cassie closed her eyes. She let the music wash over her and tried to remember what it felt like to be not a witch but just a girl.

Then she opened her eyes for a little peek at Adam. He

was beautiful. In the pale moonlight, his hair appeared auburn and his eyes darkened to a deep navy that matched the night sky. How was it possible that this boy was in love with her, and only her? The Cassie from last year would never have believed it.

She glanced at her own reflection in the car's side-view mirror. She didn't even look like the self she knew in California. Back then, she'd always felt so average. Average height, average build, ordinary brown hair. But now Cassie noticed her own multicoloured highlights, and how big and round her greyish-blue eyes were. And most importantly, she recognised how she'd matured into her power. She was confident now in a way she never could have imagined.

When they pulled up to Number Twelve, the last house on the bluff, Cassie remembered the first time she'd seen it, how frightening and old it appeared to her with its sloping roof and weathered grey clapboard siding. Was it a good thing that she'd grown so used to it, and to all the old houses on Crowhaven Road? Everything that had struck her as odd and a little creepy before had become normal to her – it had become her life.

Adam cut the engine and turned to Cassie with eager eyes.

'Just ignore her,' he said.

'Who?'

'Faye. What she said about you winning the battle but her winning the war – you can't let that get to you. She's always saying that about everything. If there were a Faye doll, when you pulled its string that's what it would say . . .' He made his voice husky like Faye's. 'Win the battle, lose the war.'

Cassie had to laugh at this.

Adam took her hands into his, obviously pleased he'd got her to smile. 'You came up with a great solution for the Master Tools,' he said. 'How did you think of it?'

'I don't know. It was weird,' Cassie said. 'It just came to me out of nowhere.'

'Not out of nowhere,' Adam said. 'From here.' He pointed to her heart. 'And here,' he said, pointing to her head. 'That's why we voted you leader. When are you going to get used to it, Cassie? You're special.'

At that moment, Cassie was so grateful to have Adam at her side. Sure, he'd voted with Diana earlier, but when Cassie spoke up, he supported her, and that's what mattered. She leaned in for a kiss from his full red lips.

Kissing him never got old. But he interpreted this one

sweet kiss goodbye as an invitation for another make-out session. He hurriedly undid his seat belt and tossed it aside.

'No,' Cassie said. 'Not again.'

Adam raised his eyebrows like a sad puppy.

'The light's on in the dining room.' Cassie tousled his hair and then pushed him away. 'Which means my mom is probably watching us right now.'

Adam grabbed for her playfully with a look of mischief in his eyes. 'One day, my love, you will care less about what people think.'

She gave him one last kiss on his smooth cheek and ran for the house before she changed her mind.

Once inside, Cassie found her mother seated at the large mahogany dining room table. There was a soothing warmth to the dimly lit room. For once, Cassie appreciated her grandfather's ancient electrical work, shoddy as it was. The golden maize-coloured walls would have appeared yellow under the unforgiving brightness of modern lighting.

Her mother's dark head of hair shot up and she smiled wide with surprise. Apparently she hadn't been watching them in the car at all, thank goodness.

'Cassie, I didn't expect you home so early,' her mom said. 'Care to help?'

Cassie surveyed the scattered piles of coloured tissue paper strewn across the vast table. 'What is all this?'

Her mother raised up both hands like she was in over her head. 'Daffodils and cranes. Decorations for the spring festival. I volunteered, but I have no idea why. Now I'm drowning in tissue paper.'

After seeing her mother sick in bed for so long, night after night, watching Melanie's great-aunt Constance feed her healing herbs and rub her down with medicinal poultices, it was a pleasure to find her mother so worked up over such an inconsequential task. And it was good to see her getting involved in a community event, too. Cassie wanted her mom to feel at home here in New Salem and to have friends, especially now that Grandma wasn't around.

'Where do I begin?' Cassie asked as she joined her mother at the regal table. She gathered stacks of yellow and green tissue paper, figuring the daffodils were easier to make than the cranes. As she began folding and fluffing the fine paper into petals, she thought to herself: *There's probably a magic way to get this done much faster*. But she was so happy and relieved to have her mom back to her old self that she didn't mind if it took all night.

'So,' her mother said, focusing her eyes fully on Cassie at last. 'How's Adam?'

Cassie felt her cheeks get warm. 'He's good.'

'And your friends?'

'They're good, too.'

Her mom dropped the silver crane she'd been struggling with and studied Cassie's face.

'You know, I'm really proud of you,' she said. 'You recovered so quickly from . . .' She paused.

'From all the drama?'

'The drama, yes, I guess you could call it that.' Her mother tried to smile.

Cassie hesitated for only a moment, but it was enough to catch her mother's attention. 'Something's wrong,' she said. 'What is it?'

Anxiety flooded Cassie's stomach. She was enjoying this bonding time and didn't want to ruin it. But her mother seemed genuinely open to talking tonight. For the first time in Cassie's life, it seemed like all the secrets between them were finally out in the open and their relationship had a clean slate. *A new beginning*, Cassie thought. That's what they were celebrating, right? That's what all these dumb paper cranes and daffodils were for, after all.

Cassie took a deep breath and looked carefully into her mother's eyes. 'I've been wondering about my dad,' she said.

Her mother immediately stiffened. Cassie noticed her jaw tighten and then she took a long sip of her tea. The cup shook almost imperceptibly in her hand. Cassie was instantly sorry she'd said it. But when her mother set her cup of tea back down, she seemed to have recovered from the shock of the question. Or at least, she was trying to appear as though she'd recovered from it.

When she finally spoke, the words came out stilted, but patient and kind. 'I'm happy to tell you anything you want to know,' she said. 'All you have to do is ask.'

Relief settled into Cassie's shoulders. It occurred to her how long she'd been keeping her worries and questions tightly wound up within her body. She pushed herself to continue talking.

'I know he – I mean, Black John – was evil,' Cassie said. 'But he's a part of me. And it's a part I feel I need to understand. Is there anything you can tell me about him?'

There. She said it. It was out in the open.

Her mother focused hard on the paper crane in her hands. 'You're absolutely right,' she said, but she didn't answer the question, and she didn't look at Cassie when she said it.

Cassie watched her mother in careful silence. She honed in much too closely on the silver crane she was holding, folding and refolding it several times.

'The problem is that they make this paper much too thin and flimsy,' she said. 'It falls apart the second you touch it.'

Right before Cassie's eyes, her mother had completely checked out of their conversation. But Cassie was determined to not give up that easily and, after a few minutes of heavy staring on Cassie's part, her mother stopped ignoring her and briefly looked up.

'Is there something you want to ask me right now?' she asked with a feigned nonchalance.

The look in her mother's eyes revealed a fear Cassie hadn't seen in her since she'd fallen ill. Her face turned pale and ghostlike, like she'd aged twenty years in those five seconds of silence. And, Cassie noticed, the silver tissue paper she held in her hand wrinkled and cracked beneath the crushing tension of her fingers, like she was squeezing it for dear life.

It was all too much for Cassie to handle. Her mother had just started feeling better. She'd just started to participate in life again. Cassie couldn't afford to wreck all that with her selfish questions. Her mother was fragile, far more fragile than Cassie ever would be.

'Never mind,' Cassie said. 'We can talk about all that another time. We have a lot to get done here.'

It had always been this way. Cassie was always the one who had to be the adult in their relationship, the one to keep her questions to herself because her mother couldn't bear the answers – or the truth. She was a fool to think it could be any different.

Chapter Three

'Spring is in the air,' Melanie said to Cassie and Laurel, closing her grey eyes momentarily and taking a deep breath in. 'You can almost smell it, can't you?'

Cassie slammed her locker shut and inhaled, but all she could smell was the same school hallway scent of sweat, paper and ammonia.

'It was a rough winter,' Laurel said. 'I think that has something to do with it.' She had adorned herself appropriately this morning in a floral-print dress. 'The spring equinox festival is going to be huge this year.'

There was a bustling excitement to their surroundings – voices seemed louder, footsteps quicker, everyone appeared more lively and animated – everyone had spring fever. Then Cassie remembered that the new principal was being announced at this morning's assembly. Maybe that was the source of all the new energy in the air? She was eager to meet the man who would be in charge of their school, especially after their last principal turned out to be Black John in disguise. But Melanie and Laurel were probably right – it was this weekend's spring festival that had everyone keyed up. Their schoolmates were all planning their outfits and debating over who'd be a worthy date. Nobody cared who the new principal was.

'It's a good sign,' Melanie said. 'A celebration of new beginnings is just what this town needs.'

Cassie wanted to be as excited as everyone about the coming spring, but her heart felt heavy in her chest. Her disastrous attempt to talk to her mother the previous night was still weighing on her.

Just then Chris and Doug Henderson swept by on rollerblades, laughing as they tore through the crowded hallway. Their forward momentum blew their dishevelled blond hair back from their identical blue-green eyes. They slowed down only to hand out star-shaped flowers to whichever pretty girls they passed. Suzan, carrying a wicker basket full of the flowers, jogged behind them to keep them supplied.

'What the heck was that?' Cassie asked.

'*Chionodoxa luciliae,*' Laurel said.

Melanie gave Laurel a shove. 'In English.'

'Sorry.' Laurel smiled. 'Those blue flowers. They're called glory-of-the-snow. They're one of the first signs of spring.'

It occurred to Cassie then that even the Henderson twins, who'd lost their sister, Kori, just last autumn, were embracing the new season. She could try a little harder to have a more positive outlook. 'I think I've seen those flowers,' she said. 'They're in the rock garden behind the gymnasium.'

'Not any more they're not,' Sean said, laughing loudly. He walked towards them with a bouquet of the blue flowers in his skinny outstretched hand and hesitantly offered them to Cassie.

'Thanks, Sean,' Cassie said, but before she could accept the bouquet, Faye stepped in and swiped it from Sean's hand. She sniffed at the buds and then shoved them back onto Sean's chest. 'Run along to the assembly and find some other pathetic girl to give those to,' she said. Then she turned to Cassie. 'I need a word with you.'

Faye was wearing all black, as she often did, but her outfit today was tighter and more revealing than usual. Cassie gave a nod to Melanie and Laurel. 'It's okay,' she said. 'Go ahead to the auditorium. I'll see you there.'

She'd promised herself she would show no fear to Faye, no matter what. She couldn't allow herself to be afraid to be alone with her, especially at school, where it was safe to assume she'd be protected from any abuse Faye could inflict upon her.

Faye, of course, wasted no time making her point. 'I know you're new to this whole leader thing,' she told Cassie. 'But even you should recognise you won't be able to play fair for long.'

'I don't know what you're talking about.'

Faye scoffed, like it was beneath her to have to explain herself. 'Don't play innocent with me, Cassie. It doesn't work.'

Cassie glanced up and down the empty hallway and put her hands on her hips. 'If you actually have something to say to me, Faye, then say it. But if you're just trying to intimidate me, you're not succeeding.'

'Liar.' Faye reached out to lightly brush aside the few strands of hair that had fallen in front of Cassie's eyes, and Cassie jumped back.

Faye smiled. 'Here's what I have to say. Power always creates enemies. It divides people into two types, good and bad. If you really want to be a leader of this Circle, then you need to pick a side.'

Cassie remembered Diana once saying that power was only power – it wasn't good or bad. *Only the way we use it is good or bad*, she'd said. But even Diana had changed her opinion about this.

'I've already chosen a side,' Cassie said.

The star ruby around Faye's neck glistened. It was the same colour as her lipstick. 'No, you haven't,' she said. 'There's something in you that proves you're daddy's little girl. You can feel it inside you. A darkness. I know you can.'

Cassie hugged her books tighter to her chest. 'You don't know anything.'

'Isn't it exhausting trying so hard to emulate Diana when really you're just like me?'

'No. Because I'm nothing like you.'

Faye let out a deep, throaty laugh and took a step back. She'd accomplished what she'd intended. Cassie was significantly rattled.

'Better hurry up,' she said. 'You don't want to be late to the assembly.' She pulled a tube of lipstick from her bag and applied another slash of dark pigment to her lips. 'Want some?' She held the blood-red tube out to Cassie. 'I think it's your colour.'

In a flash of anger Cassie thought to swat the lipstick right out of Faye's hand. But that would be giving her exactly what she wanted. She was trying to push Cassie into giving in to her lowest impulses, to be as brash and reckless as she was.

But Cassie wouldn't do it. She wouldn't give Faye that satisfaction. Instead, she turned her back on her and, when she did, she caught sight of someone she hadn't seen before. A boy. Faye noticed him, too.

Together, they watched him walk up the hallway. He was tall and muscular with light-brown hair, and he must have just finished working out, because he was wearing warm-ups and sneakers. He carried a gym bag in one hand and a lacrosse stick in the other.

'That boy is gorgeous.' Faye capped her lipstick and stuffed it into her purse. 'You know how I love those sweaty jocks.'

Cassie rolled her eyes.

Faye immediately approached the boy to stake her claim. 'Are you lost?' she called out to him. 'I can help you find your way.'

His head shot up when he realised he was being spoken to. Cassie saw that his eyes were green like emeralds, as beautiful as Diana's.

'No, thank you,' he said, in a voice both rugged and cocky. 'I know where I'm heading.'

'To that boring assembly?' Faye wasn't about to give up that easy. 'In that case, I can help you lose your way.'

That got a smile out of him, but he directed it at Cassie. 'Hi,' he said. 'I'm Max.'

'This is Faye,' Cassie said, returning Max's grin. 'She's glad to meet you.'

Max dropped his gym bag onto the floor and shook Faye's hand in a way that made it obvious he was used to girls fawning over him.

'Cassie,' Faye said, still holding Max's thick hand in hers. 'Won't Adam be waiting for you at the assembly? You should probably get going.'

Cassie nodded. 'She's right. I should.'

As Cassie turned away, she heard Max call after her, 'See you in there.'

Cassie made it into the auditorium just in time for the welcoming ceremony. She was relieved to find Adam waving her over to where he was seated in the last row. The auditorium was more crowded than she had ever seen it. Groups of students were crammed in the back and up each exit row. The humming excitement Cassie picked up on in the hallway had carried over here, where it heightened like rough water constrained by a dam. But once Mr Humphries tapped on the microphone to quiet the crowd and make some announcements, that restless energy died down to a low-level boredom. Assemblies were always fun until the assembly part.

Cassie let her eyes roam over the crowd. She found Diana all the way up front, seated with her AP English class. Melanie and Laurel had joined Suzan, Sean and the Henderson brothers in the centre rows about midway from the stage. And Deborah and Nick were just a few rows behind them. Cassie noticed that none of them looked concerned. They appeared as bored and apathetic as the rest of the school. Was she the only one still reeling from the last assembly they had had to welcome a principal? Were they all just faking it, trying to put their best faces forward? Or was everyone really that much better at moving on than Cassie?

Sally Waltman and Portia Bainbridge were sitting in their cluster of cheerleaders. Sally's rust-coloured hair stood out from the rest of her mostly blonde friends, so she was easy to spot in their crowd. She was laughing at something Portia was saying, probably making fun of someone, like she always did. The Circle had come to an uneasy truce with Portia and her brothers, but Cassie still didn't like her.

The Divide

'You okay?' Adam asked when Cassie settled into her seat. 'You've got that I-just-had-a-Faye-encounter look.'

'I'm fine. Faye was getting up in my face, but then a hot boy walked by and she forgot all about me.'

'That's our Faye.' Adam took Cassie's hand in his and squeezed it. 'Who was the boy?'

'I don't know, someone new. His name was Max.'

Cassie searched the auditorium for Faye and found her standing in the corner talking to Max – talking *at* him was more like it. He leaned with both hands on his lacrosse stick, like he might fall over from boredom if it weren't holding him up.

Cassie shifted her attention to the man she assumed was the new principal waiting off to the side. He wore a finely cut dark suit and had salt-and-pepper hair. He was tall, with broad shoulders, and kept his hands clasped behind his back. He was handsome, the way Mr Brunswick had been handsome.

Weak applause welcomed him to the stage. 'Thank you,' he said as he adjusted the microphone. 'I'm Mr Boylan, and it's a pleasure to make your acquaintance.'

His voice was deeper than Cassie had expected it to be. His outer appearance was dapper and elegant, but he had

29

the voice of a lumberjack – it had a toughness to it, a grit, and the slightest hint of an accent she couldn't place.

A shiver ran down her spine.

No, Cassie thought to herself. *You're being paranoid. Just because Mr Brunswick turned out to be evil doesn't mean Mr Boylan will.* She figured she must have been suffering from some kind of post-traumatic stress, the way soldiers returned from wars startled at every harmless loud sound they heard.

But as Mr Boylan continued speaking, every muscle in Cassie's body tightened in defence. She glanced at Adam to see if he sensed anything off about the principal, too, but he was calmly watching the stage with no expression of alarm.

'Thank you all for your gracious welcome,' Mr Boylan said. 'I hope you'll do the same for my son, who will also be a student here.' He pointed to the far corner, where Max was still leaning on his lacrosse stick, staring straight ahead.

Adam and Cassie looked at each other simultaneously. Neither of them had to say it.

Of course. Faye's new crush was the principal's son.

Faye was smirking behind him, watching the back of his head as if she could burn a hole through it with her desire. When she caught Cassie watching, she puckered her lips into a kiss and blew it Cassie's way. Then she stuck out her tongue, pretending she might lick the back of Max's neck.

'This can't be good,' Cassie said.

Chapter Four

As she walked home from school that afternoon, Cassie finally had a moment to herself to think. Diana and some of the others were going into town to shop for spring festival outfits. *You need a spring dress for the spring festival*, Suzan had insisted when Cassie said she was feeling too tired to shop. But Diana interjected on Cassie's behalf, saying if she was tired it was best to rest.

Did that mean Diana didn't really want her there? Cassie wished she was feeling more confident about her friendship with Diana, but it seemed out of sorts, just like everything right now.

Cassie decided to walk the longer, more scenic route home along Cherry Hill Road, where rows of Kwanzan and dwarf bing cherry trees would be on the brink of blooming. It was a blustery March day and the sound of the wind in the trees was her favourite. She stopped walking for a moment to look up at their leaves, to watch them shake and dance overhead until she was dizzy.

'This is my turf,' a voice behind her said.

She glanced around and saw a black leather jacket and black jeans.

'Nick,' she said. 'I walked this way to be alone, so maybe you're on my turf.' She was trying to sound playfully sarcastic. Then she immediately ruined it by adding, 'But it's really nice to run into you.'

She noticed him shift uncomfortably at the sappy comment, but more of the same started sputtering from her mouth. 'It's just . . . we've hardly got to talk lately,' she said. 'And we never hang out any more.'

Nick's face appeared cold. No smile, not even a hint of one. He obviously didn't feel the same way. He looked away and patted his jacket pocket for his cigarettes. Then he remembered he'd quit, so he stopped patting and stood still.

'I miss you, Nick,' Cassie heard herself say. And she immediately wished it hadn't come out sounding so needy and pathetic.

Nick had been this way – aloof and closed off – since Cassie and Adam got together. The rational part of her brain knew he was only shutting her out because he'd been hurt, but the other part of her brain, the irrational part, didn't care at all about that and just wanted him back in her life.

She touched the soft leather of his jacket and asked, as innocently as she could, 'Don't you miss me at all?'

A pang of agony shot across his face, like she'd stabbed him in the stomach with a sharp knife.

'Cassie,' he said.

He was about to say something important. She could tell by the gentle tone of his voice and the way he was struggling to find the right words. It was so difficult for him to express his emotions that to watch him working so hard at it now made Cassie's heart melt a little. This was the tender side of Nick not many people had access to.

'Cassie, listen,' he said.

But just then Adam drove up, honking his horn. 'Hey, you two,' he called out. 'Want a ride?'

Shoot. What terrible timing. She and Nick were finally getting somewhere.

But the moment was lost. Nick's face, which had opened itself up briefly, closed again, tighter and more secure than a vault.

'Do you want a ride home?' Cassie feebly asked him.

The sight of her with Adam was the last thing Nick needed, and Cassie knew it. 'I'll pass,' he said, with the coldest voice he could muster. 'But you'd better go,' he added, when he noticed Cassie's hesitation. 'Your chariot awaits.'

Cassie was torn. For a split second she imagined their alternate future, the one where Adam didn't pull up, where she and Nick talked the whole long walk home beneath a canopy of trees. She didn't want to let this possibility go. But she knew not to push Nick too far. After all, her loyalties were to Adam, and they always would be.

Nick started shuffling away in the opposite direction of home. Cassie rushed to catch up with him and whispered into his ear. 'You may have earned the right to wallow a bit,' she said. 'But I'm not going to let you go that easily.'

Then she jogged back to Adam's car, opened the door, and climbed inside.

The interior of Adam's car always smelled the same. It was the sweet musk of autumn leaves and gasoline, oiled leather and rubber, and it never failed to make Cassie feel a charge.

Adam looked her over, analysing every inch of her face with his piercing blue eyes. 'I thought you were

35

going out dress shopping with the girls.'

'I didn't feel like it.'

He rested his warm hand on her knee. 'Cassie, are you sure everything's okay?'

She gazed out the window and didn't answer.

'Was Nick giving you a hard time back there?'

'What? No, of course not. If anything, I was giving him a hard time, trying to get him to be my friend again.'

Adam returned his hand to the steering wheel and gripped it so tightly, his knuckles whitened. 'He needs time.'

'I know.'

Cassie watched the more ordinary streets of New Salem give way to Crowhaven Road and decided to change the subject.

'Did you get a weird feeling from the new principal today?' she asked.

'No, why? Did you?'

'Kind of, but I'm not sure,' Cassie said honestly. 'I think I want to ask Constance about it. Maybe she knows a spell or something that can show us his true nature.'

Adam tried to suppress a smile. 'I think you're being a little paranoid, Cassie. Rightfully so, after all we've been through. But honestly, the only thing I found freaky about the principal is that Faye is into his son.'

'I know, you're probably right.' Cassie returned her gaze out the window. She noticed a black sedan behind theirs and strained to see if it was one of their friends. Not too many cars had a reason to turn onto Crowhaven Road.

'Cassie,' Adam said, 'listen to me. Black John isn't haunting us any more. He's gone. We won.'

In spite of all of Adam's sensitivity, it bothered Cassie that he still glossed over the fact that Black John, though evil, was her father. Whenever Adam mentioned him, it was always, *He's gone, gone forever* – which of course was a good thing, but Adam could at least acknowledge that his death was confusing for her.

'I think I'd still like to go see Constance,' she said. 'Will you drop me off there, please?'

Adam got quiet then, which meant he had the sense to know he'd said something to upset Cassie.

They were just about at Constance's house now, so he let up on the accelerator and slowed to a stop. Cassie noticed the black car behind them also stopped. It then made a sharp U-turn and headed back to the main road. *Weird*, she thought.

* * *

At first no one answered her knock, but then Cassie saw Constance's grey head of hair appear in the front window. She waved her birdlike hand at Cassie and then opened the door.

'Are you here to see Melanie?' she asked. 'She's not home from school yet.'

'Actually, Aunt Constance, I came to talk to you.'

'Uh-oh. What's wrong?' She led Cassie across the spotless hardwood floor to the parlour, where she'd been having tea.

Cassie had grown quite comfortable in this house since her mother had stayed there when she was ill. It was similar to Cassie's own home, but in much better shape. The walls were freshly painted, the silver was polished to a shine, and there wasn't a speck of dust anywhere. The parlour smelled like the oil soap used to clean wood.

Constance refilled her willow-patterned teacup and poured a cup for Cassie. Then she sat back in her large rocking chair. 'What's on your mind?' she asked.

'Nothing, really,' Cassie said. 'I guess I just came to ask your advice.'

'About what?' Constance was thin and regal, but she looked almost childlike, rocking back and forth in her chair.

'I've been feeling kind of uneasy lately,' Cassie said.

Constance stopped the rocking and rested her feet flat on the floor. 'You'll have to be more specific if advice is what you want, dear.'

'Believe it or not, I'm really trying.' Cassie set her teacup down. 'I guess part of it is that I know I should be happy. The Circle defeated Black John, and my mother is well again. And I have Adam, who loves me very much.'

'But?'

'But I can't seem to relax.' Cassie leaned in close to Constance and began speaking more softly. 'Like today, when our new principal was introduced. I started to feel all shaky, right there at the assembly. I know it wasn't about him, but how do I know, or how can I tell . . . Oh, I don't know.'

'How can you tell the difference between instinct and anxiety?' Constance smiled.

Cassie nodded.

'There's only one way,' Constance said. 'Years of practice. That's one of the biggest challenges of having the sight.'

She leaned back in her chair and appeared lost in her own thoughts for a moment. Then her thin red lips formed a smile.

'Your grandmother was the same way,' she said. 'What you call nervous. If you only knew how many times she woke me up from a sound sleep, crying about a bad omen that turned out to be indigestion.'

Constance started laughing so hard, tears formed in the corners of her eyes. She reached for a tissue and patted them away before she went on. 'I'm sorry, I don't mean to make light of it. But it'll get easier with time, Cassie, you can be sure of that.'

'So what you're saying is there's no magic way to know for sure who's good and who's evil, no spell to test the principal's true nature?'

Constance resisted the urge to start laughing again. 'Honey, if only that spell did exist, it would have been the first one I showed you.' She looked at Cassie lovingly. 'Unfortunately, there's no shortcut to peace of mind.'

When Cassie made no reply, wrinkled lines appeared between Constance's eyebrows. 'Practise your daily meditations and your invocations,' she said. 'Cultivate tranquillity as best you can.'

It was simple advice, but Cassie left Constance's house feeling just a little bit lighter.

Chapter Five

When Cassie arrived at Old Town Hall, the sun was shining down on the carnival as booths and tables were being set up for the evening's festivities. She searched for her mom among the volunteers so she could help her put up the decorations they'd finally finished making late last night.

Old Town Hall was one of the earliest municipal buildings in New Salem. When it had been in use, it housed all the town's federal offices. The surrounding area was designed to be an outdoor market, but these days it was mostly used as a public art space and, of course, to host yearly spring and fall festivals.

'Hey, Cassie.' Laurel appeared carrying a tray of tulip bulbs that was nearly twice her size. She dropped it onto a nearby table and waved a few sweaty strands of hair away from her pixie-like face. 'Are you psyched for tonight's festival?'

'Sure,' Cassie said unconvincingly.

'Well, you should be,' Laurel said. 'The spring equinox is important to us as witches.' She looked to her left and then to her right to be sure nobody had heard her. And then, as Cassie expected, she launched into a history lesson. History and botany lessons were pretty much mandatory when talking to Laurel. You either loved her for it or you had the urge to tape her mouth shut, but for now Cassie humoured her.

'Like many traditions in New Salem, the origin of the spring festival has roots in paganism,' Laurel said. 'This festival used to be called Ostara's Festival, and it was a holiday to celebrate the Goddess waking from her winter slumber. It was a time when our ancestors honoured the balance of all things, the physical with the spiritual. The old books said it was a time to plant seeds in the garden, as well as a time to plant the seeds of desired manifestation.'

'But what does that mean?' Cassie asked.

'It means it's a time to start new projects and put new plans into action.' Laurel picked up her tray with a grunt and began to walk away. 'It's something to get excited about,' she said over her shoulder.

The Divide

Cassie let her eyes wander around the square. In every booth was a local merchant offering samples of food or drink, or the chance to bid on some item up for auction. Local bands were setting up their equipment on a ramshackle stage. The whole event had simply become a backdrop for the kick-off of the tourist season. But still, Cassie thought she should embrace it. It was a celebration of sorts, like Laurel said.

Cassie found her mother on the far side of the square, stapling paper daffodils along a wooden baseboard. Across from her, Cassie saw Melanie and Constance setting up their jewellery booth. Melanie's smooth cap of chestnut hair was pulled neatly back, while Constance's grey mane feathered madly in the wind. They were quite a pair; Melanie was tall and beautiful and prepossessing, and Constance was shrunken and slumped over, bossily calling out commands with her wrinkled pointer finger. But the love and compassion between them was palpable, and the jewellery they designed was a physical product of that love. Melanie had told Cassie that the local townspeople didn't have a real understanding of crystals, but that didn't matter. Their jewellery made for pretty conversation pieces, and Aunt Constance really appreciated the extra cash.

Cassie waved to Melanie from afar and then spotted

Diana. She was wearing all white, and the way the sun was striking her blonde hair, it appeared almost white, too. *My God*, Cassie thought, *Diana is literally shimmering like an angel*. And appropriately, she was helping with the charity raffle this year. In fact, she'd organised it. Sometimes Cassie wondered if there was anything Diana couldn't do.

Cassie gave her mom a signal to let her know she'd be right there and then headed over to the raffle table to say hello to Diana. She'd felt so distant from Diana lately, she thought stopping by would be a nice gesture. Maybe even a first step in clearing the air between them.

Cassie understood the distance was because she spent most of her free time with Adam these days. How could that not make things weird, when not so long ago it used to be Diana who spent all her time with Adam?

But in spite of all that, when Diana noticed Cassie coming her way now, she couldn't have offered her a more heartfelt greeting. She dropped her clipboard onto the table and jogged across the square to meet Cassie halfway.

'I'm so glad you're here,' she said. 'Your mother's decorations look fantastic.'

'Thanks,' Cassie said, and then hesitated. She hadn't

known she was going to do this, but in the moment it felt right. 'Can we talk?' she asked.

Without waiting for an answer, she took Diana's hand tightly in her own and led her to the side of the square, where there was a long stone bench they could sit on without the risk of anyone overhearing their conversation. 'There's something I have to tell you,' Cassie said.

Diana's green eyes narrowed with concern, but she sat down, as instructed. Cassie sat across from her, anxiously rubbing her fingers along the bench's stone surface.

'I've been feeling so bad,' she said. 'For all the awkwardness.'

Diana smiled wide. 'Kind of like right now?'

'Yeah.' Cassie felt herself blush. 'I guess I am being kind of awkward right now. It's just that I know how close you and Adam were, and the sacrifice you made, and—'

Diana cut Cassie off mid-sentence. 'Cassie, I know. I really do. And it has been hard at times, but I think we've all grown used to it a lot faster than you have.'

She put her hands on Cassie's shoulders and gave her a little shake. 'There are no hard feelings. Honestly. It's you who's making it hard, for yourself.'

Cassie's eyes filled with tears and she realised Diana

was right. She had been making things unnecessarily difficult. This was supposed to be a new beginning. Everywhere around her, people were embracing change while she clung on to old hurts and past fears.

'Does this mean we can hang out more?' she asked.

'I sure hope so!' Diana brought her in for a hug and, when Cassie closed her eyes, everything felt just right. *A new beginning*, she thought to herself again. Now she really would be able to enjoy the festival.

Together she and Diana walked through the square, arm in arm, back to the raffle table. Cassie didn't want their renewed closeness to end, but she had work to do.

'I'd better go help my mom,' she said, and was about to walk away when a girl approached her. The girl had long waves of bright-red hair and wore high black boots that caught on the hem of her slip dress.

'Excuse me,' she said. 'I'm looking for the bed-and-breakfast that's supposed to be right around here.' She was about the same height and build as Cassie, and her eyes were a very dark brown, almost black.

Diana pointed west. 'It's about a two-minute walk that way.'

The girl gripped the handle of her overstuffed suitcase and stood gawking at them, as if she were hoping

46

for more. 'I'm Scarlett,' she said, offering her free hand to Diana.

Diana introduced herself and Cassie, and then asked, 'Are you visiting from out of town?'

'Not visiting. I just moved here.' Scarlett bit at her fingernail, which was covered in chipped black nail polish. 'I'm only staying at the B and B for now, if I ever find it.'

Diana raised her eyebrows. 'Moving to a new town with only one suitcase, that's very impressive.'

Scarlett laughed uncomfortably like she wasn't sure if Diana was playfully teasing or rudely making fun of her. Cassie wasn't entirely sure either. She knew Diana well enough to sense that she had her guard up around this stranger.

'Will you be going to New Salem High?' Diana asked.

Scarlett shook her head. 'I graduated early. I'm working on the docks for the summer.'

'I see,' Diana said, in a tone dripping with judgement.

Diana got like this around Outsiders sometimes. Cassie knew she didn't mean to be impolite; in fact, she probably wasn't even aware of it. It was an unconscious self-righteousness that came from always knowing she was special. But Cassie knew what growing up average was like, and she'd once been the new girl in town. She sympathised with how awful and alienated Scarlett probably felt right now.

'Well, thank you for the directions,' Scarlett said. 'It was nice meeting you.'

'Wait.' Cassie had the sudden urge to remedy Diana's inhospitable welcome. 'You should come to the festival tonight. It's right here; you can't miss it.'

Scarlett giggled in a way that made her sound like a little girl, and Cassie couldn't help but join in. There was something refreshing about her. 'We just met and already you're taking a shot at my poor sense of direction?' Then her face warmed. 'I'd love to come, thank you.'

'Great,' Cassie said. 'Then we'll see you later.'

Cassie watched Scarlett walk away, and Diana picked up her clipboard from the table. 'That was neighbourly of you,' she said.

'What do you mean?'

'You know.' Diana scrutinised her list of things to do, flipping through its many pages. 'Considerate, gregarious.'

'I know what neighbourly means, but what do *you* mean?'

Diana set the clipboard down and rolled her pen back and forth in her fingers while analysing Cassie's expression. 'You saw something in her, didn't you? What was it?'

Cassie should have known there was never getting anything past Diana. It was true, she had seen something in Scarlett, but she wasn't sure what.

Cassie felt a tingle travel up her spine and down her arms, all the way to her fingers. It was an excitement she couldn't place. 'I'm really not sure. But I think it was something good.'

'Well, that's pleasant news for a change,' Diana said.

'Tell me about it.'

'Maybe it was her hair dye drawing you in.'

'Be nice,' Cassie said.

'I'm not being mean,' Diana said naughtily. 'It made me want to drink a glass of wild cherry Kool-Aid. I love that stuff.' Then the two of them broke into loud, uninhibited laughter, the way they used to.

Chapter Six

The moon overhead was a bright white waxing crescent and the sky was clear. Cassie and Adam were standing by the maypole hand in hand, and she felt radiant in the yellow camisole dress her friends picked out for her. She'd found it in the dining room early that morning. Suzan had dropped it off with a note written in her loopy script: *This dress screamed your name!*

Suzan had also bought ties for all the guys, and they looked good, but the girls outshone them in their dresses. Melanie was in green chiffon and Laurel in carnation-pink voile. Suzan, always voluptuous, had chosen a copper-coloured tank dress for herself that was pushing the boundary of indecent exposure. Diana wore an under-stated ivory silk tunic.

Deborah, who rarely wore dresses, was decked out in

her own way. She had on tight white jeans, a white T-shirt, and a purple leather jacket. 'Have you seen Faye?' she asked Cassie and Adam.

Adam shrugged his shoulders, but Sean responded, 'She's out on the lookout for Max.'

Deborah scoffed. 'She hasn't given up on him yet? He's been evading her all week.'

Sean shook his head. 'Not a chance,' he said. 'Faye never backs down that easily.'

'What about Nick?' Cassie asked. 'Have you seen him?'

Deborah's face hardened at the question. When it came to Cassie, she was extremely protective of her cousin. 'I don't think he's coming.'

'Why not?' Cassie asked.

'Because he's not.' Deborah tried to stare Cassie down, but Cassie brushed it off. Deborah thought she was doing the right thing, guarding Nick from getting hurt any more than he already had, but she didn't understand that Cassie's intentions were good. After clearing the air with Diana, she'd felt so much better. She hoped to do the same with Nick tonight.

Diana frowned at Deborah in a way that revealed she sympathised with Cassie's predicament. 'Nick may show,' she said. 'If he's anything, he's unpredictable.'

There was a moment of silence as Cassie let her eyes wander up the maypole. She admired the multicoloured garlands and ribbons streaming down from its apex. Then Diana said, 'Hey, Cassie, isn't that Scarlett?'

Scarlett had spotted them and was making her way through the crowd in their direction. She was wearing a cornflower-blue baby-doll dress and her long red hair was stuffed beneath a brown felt bowler hat. She waved when her eyes locked with Cassie's and then she picked up her pace to a trot.

'Who is that?' Adam asked.

Cassie noticed a shard of fascinated curiosity in Adam's voice.

'Ooh, I love that hat,' Suzan said.

Deborah nodded. She always appreciated a girl stylish enough to successfully pull off wearing an article of men's clothing. 'Those boots are killer, too,' she said.

Scarlett was all smiles and confidence as Cassie introduced her to the rest of the group. Her dark eyes passed over each of them individually and she greeted everyone with the affection of an old friend.

It wasn't just Scarlett's fashion sense that was captivating, Cassie noted. It was her nature; she was immediately comfortable with everyone she met. And she was pretty. Sean's tongue was practically hanging out of his mouth when he shook her hand.

Scarlett extracted herself from Sean's grasp with a chuckle and turned to Diana.

'Good to see you again,' she said.

'Yes,' Diana answered, in a way that made Cassie cringe. But Scarlett flashed a white smile that showed she refused to take Diana's indifference to heart.

'The egg toss is starting,' Sean said excitedly, trying to regain Scarlett's attention. 'We should go cheer on Chris and Doug. The grand prize is a five-hundred-dollar gift certificate to Pete's Candy Store, and they're determined to win it.'

Scarlett scanned the many booths and food trucks. 'Actually,' she said, 'I'm famished. And I'm dying for one of those chorizo skewers.'

'I'll come with you,' Cassie said. She was anxious to learn more about Scarlett and, come to think of it, she was pretty hungry herself.

The group split up then, everyone heading over to the egg-toss lawn, except for Adam and Diana, who were on their way to visit Melanie and Constance at their jewellery booth.

Cassie and Scarlett each bought a skewer and struggled

to not talk with their mouths full as they walked the festival's perimeter. 'So you're staying at the B and B?' Cassie asked as innocently as possible.

Scarlett nodded, chewed and swallowed.

'Where are your parents?'

'My mom passed away,' Scarlett said abruptly, like she wanted to get that information out of the way as fast as possible.

'Oh, I'm sorry.'

'She grew up here,' Scarlett continued. 'That's why I wanted to come to New Salem, to kind of reconnect with her, and my past.' She looked away then, perhaps afraid she was oversharing.

Cassie searched her mind for the right thing to say. 'I think that's great. I mean, I think that's a really brave thing to do. Even if it's painful.'

Scarlett nodded. 'I guess I'm just looking for a new start.'

'I know what you mean,' Cassie said.

'So tell me something about you.'

Cassie's mind raced. She wanted to change the subject to something less heavy, but it occurred to her that every good and exciting thing she wanted to tell also involved the Circle, so she was left speechless.

For the first time since she moved to New Salem, she understood why being friends with an Outsider could be such a challenge.

'Well,' Cassie said, 'that's my mother over there selling raffle tickets.' But when she pointed her mother out, she also caught sight of Adam and Diana off in the corner, sharing a vanilla ice-cream cone. They were laughing because Adam had gotten ice cream on his nose and chin, and the more he tried to wipe it away, the more ice cream he smeared around.

Cassie felt her stomach drop. But why? It was only an ice-cream cone. A shared snack between friends was nothing to get upset over. She would just join them. She led Scarlett their way and then noticed Faye approaching from the opposite direction.

Faye was wearing a sheer black dress that fit her like a corset. A few paces behind her was Max, who, even in his casual polo shirt, still looked like he'd just stepped out of an Abercrombie catalogue.

Adam and Diana stopped laughing and regained control of their ice-cream situation once they noticed Cassie and the others heading their way.

Faye introduced Max and then sized up Scarlett. 'Who are you?' she asked.

'This is Scarlett,' Cassie said. 'She's new to town, just like you, Max.'

Max gave a nod to Scarlett, but his focus was clearly on Diana. 'I saw you at the assembly on Friday,' he said. 'You were the only one paying attention to my dad's boring speech.'

Diana appeared flustered. 'You saw me?' she said, and then added, 'It wasn't boring.'

'No? Are you sure?' Max stared at her roguishly until she cracked.

'Okay, maybe just a little.'

'Thank you for your honesty.' Max reached for Diana's hand and squeezed it between his thick fingers. 'Now we can be friends.'

Diana blushed, and Cassie noticed Adam shift uncomfortably.

'My dad's here somewhere,' Max said, still addressing only Diana. 'If you find him, you should let him know what a great orator you think he is.'

Faye was clenching her jaw so tightly, Cassie feared her head might explode.

'I'll do that,' Diana said. 'But if you'll excuse me for right now, we were about to go cheer for our friends.' She gestured toward the egg-toss competition.

Max looked a little disappointed. 'Yeah, I should go find my dad,' he said.

Faye made a move to follow him, but he stopped her. 'I'll see you later,' he said, and then disappeared into the crowd.

Adam, who'd been deathly silent till now, had a look of disgust on his face. 'Well, that was weird.'

'Adam,' Diana scolded, 'he was just trying to fit in. That's what people do when they're new. They'll do anything to impress you.'

Scarlett looked down, assuming that was a knock at her. Cassie opened her mouth to say something, but before any words came out, Faye stormed off.

'Max wasn't working so hard to impress her,' Adam said.

'Faye's been sexually harassing him since the moment he got here,' Diana said, raising her voice. 'He doesn't have to *try* for her.'

Cassie wished Scarlett wasn't witnessing this strange moment of tension. It was actually embarrassing, how petty her friends must have appeared.

'Let's go,' she said to Scarlett. 'They'll catch up.'

Together they crossed the square. 'Diana and Adam aren't usually like that,' Cassie said. 'You just happened to catch them in a weird moment.'

'I get it.' Scarlett smiled. 'Couples get jealous; they fight.'

Suddenly Cassie felt sick again. 'Adam's my boyfriend,' she said quietly. 'Not Diana's.'

'Oh.' Scarlett bit her lip. 'That was stupid of me, I didn't realise—'

'No, it's fine. I can see why you'd think that. It's kind of complicated.'

When they found the rest of the group clustered at one end of the cheering section, Cassie was relieved for the chance to change the subject. The competition was down to Chris and Doug, and a brother-sister team who couldn't be a day over eleven years old.

'They really like candy,' Cassie said to Scarlett, as if that were a reasonable explanation.

'I can respect that,' Scarlett said. 'I really like candy, too. I once ate so many Skittles, I sneezed rainbows for three days.'

It was a dumb joke, but Cassie recognised it for what it was. Scarlett was trying to lighten things up, to comfort her, and she appreciated that. Outsider or not, she liked this girl.

Just then, a scream for help came from the north

side of the square, and everyone's attention shifted. All eyes searched for the source of the bloodcurdling sound, but the group recognised it immediately as Melanie's voice. They dashed towards the jewellery booth. Even Chris and Doug let their eggs fall to run and help.

When Cassie reached the booth, she pushed through the crowd to find Melanie's great-aunt Constance sprawled out on the ground. Melanie was crying out for someone to call an ambulance. A few townspeople with medical training kneeled over Constance, taking her vital signs, ordering everyone to stay back and give her some air. One of them had a hold on Melanie, who was thrashing and swinging at him before Diana and Laurel caught her by the arms and pulled her off to the side.

A woman who'd been about to purchase a necklace from Constance said, 'She was fine one second, and then she got this panicked look on her face and just collapsed.'

Adam eyed the crowd for anyone suspicious. Cassie searched the mass of strangers' faces for her mother but couldn't find her. Maybe she'd gone for help. Or maybe the sight of Constance dropping to the ground was too much for her. In moments of crisis her mother tended to break down rather than rise up. It wouldn't have surprised Cassie if she'd gone running home.

The paramedics arrived and Cassie had to look away while they performed CPR on Constance's unresponsive body. The group embraced Melanie while Adam hugged Cassie close. She buried her head in his shoulder.

It was impossible to know how much time passed while the paramedics worked on Constance. Cassie kept thinking it had to be a joke. *Ha ha, got you*, Cassie imagined Constance saying from her spot on the ground. Constance was always trying to remind them of the fragility of life and the delicate balance of all things. Maybe this was just one more lesson. But then the paramedics stopped their pushing and pulling and pumping and gasping. There were no more mouthfuls of air to be given or received, and there was no more hope. The paramedic in charge stood up and brought their efforts to the ultimate conclusion. He declared Aunt Constance dead. *Expired* was the word he used, which struck Cassie as unbelievably harsh.

'Probably a brain aneurysm,' he told his deputy, and then he expressed his condolences to Melanie. 'We did everything we could, miss,' he said.

Cassie had never seen Melanie lose it the way she did at that moment. She'd always kept herself together in the face of any hardship – especially in public. But this was just too much. She fell to her knees and wailed. *So much for new beginnings*, Cassie thought.

Chapter Seven

'Everyone around us dies,' Cassie said. 'No matter what.'

The scene kept playing over and over in her mind – the sound of Melanie screaming and the sight of Constance on the ground. She couldn't stop shaking. Even with all the lanterns and flickering candles surrounding her, she felt cold in the lighthouse.

Laurel wanted to perform a strength-giving ceremony to help Melanie through the next few days. They'd gathered the necessary herbs and crystals, but once they were about to begin, the group found they were hardly capable of doing anything in an organised fashion. Everyone was lost in their own fog, traumatised.

Adam draped a blanket over Cassie's shoulders, but that, too, felt chilly and damp on her body. She couldn't stop shivering.

'She needs something to help her calm down,' Adam said, and Diana quickly rummaged through the top drawer of the large pewter dresser they'd stocked with herbs and medicinal roots.

She retrieved a tiny glass bottle and eyedropper. 'This is a valerian-root tincture,' she said, holding the dropper up to Cassie's mouth. 'It'll help ease your nerves. We should all take some.'

Faye yanked Cassie away before the drops reached her tongue. 'Don't try to sedate her from the truth, Diana.' She slid her arm around Cassie's waist. 'What Cassie said is correct. Everyone around us does die. And she's right to be losing her mind a little over it.' Faye passed her eyes over each member of the group until settling on Diana. 'But I wonder if that has to be the case any more.'

Diana placed the tincture down on the table. 'What are you saying?'

'I think you know.' Faye moved to the centre of the room. 'We have the Master Tools now. The most powerful tools a witch could have. We might be able to bring Constance back.'

Diana was silent, but Laurel shot up from her seat. 'Faye's right. Constance was teaching us so much about our powers, and that was just the beginning of our training. We need her.'

Deborah nodded. 'A witch as powerful as she was should be easy to bring back.'

Diana's already pale face seemed to whiten further. 'I don't know,' she said. 'I want to save Constance, but unleashing that kind of dark magic could be dangerous. We don't know what the repercussions will be.'

'Have you all gone completely crazy?' Cassie asked. 'You actually believe we can raise the dead?'

'Actually,' Adam said, 'it's not that far-fetched. I know this is still all new to you, Cassie, but necromancy has been used since the third century.'

'There's an actual term for it?' Cassie could hardly believe it.

'It derives from the Greek,' Laurel said. 'From *nekos*, meaning dead, and *manteia*, which means divination.'

Cassie looked to Diana for confirmation, and she nodded. 'But for the Greeks, necromancy signified the descent into Hades,' Diana said. 'It was used as a way to consult the dead. It wasn't intended to actually raise the dead back into the mortal sphere.'

'But,' Adam interjected, 'we know for a fact that it

was used that way by our own ancestors. In fact, Diana, don't you—'

Diana's green eyes flared to shut Adam up. But Faye, always vigilant, picked up on it. 'Diana, don't you *what*?'

Diana rested both her slender hands on the Pembroke table in front of her. To keep from falling over, Cassie imagined. Then she spoke warily. 'There's a resuscitation spell in my Book of Shadows,' she said. 'Adam and I discovered it a few years ago.'

Faye released a moan of pure satisfaction. 'I knew it.'

'Let's do it,' Deborah said. 'We have the power and we have the spell.'

Suzan agreed. 'We have to at least try.'

Adam was quiet, but Cassie perceived a quivering excitement beneath his noncommittal expression. He wanted this – to test the limits of his power. It was the side of Adam that Cassie often forgot was there. Behind his relentlessly responsible façade, he was an adventurer at heart.

Diana, still looking weary, said, 'I suppose it is worth a try. As long as we're extremely careful. But we should put it to a vote.'

Laurel joined Faye at the centre of the room. 'I'll do the honours in Melanie's absence,' she said. 'All those in favour of saving Constance, raise your hand.'

Everyone's hand went up except Cassie's. Laurel looked at her, surprised the vote wasn't unanimous.

'I want to,' Cassie said. 'Of course I want to. I'm just . . . scared.'

'We can't do this spell without a full Circle,' Diana said. 'It's all or nothing.'

Laurel's voice took on a pleading tone. 'This is Melanie's family we're talking about. Her only family.'

But Diana was firm. 'We can't force Cassie to perform a spell of this magnitude against her will.'

Cassie felt the room's attention rotate to her. 'I'll do it,' she called out before anyone else could say anything. 'Nobody's forcing me. Constance was family to all of us, and I want to do it.'

Faye clapped her hands together and immediately began giving orders. 'We have to work fast,' she said. 'And we need the Tools. I'll go get the garter.'

She pointed to Cassie and Diana. 'You two go dig up the bracelet and diadem from wherever you hid them. And, Diana, don't forget your Book of Shadows. The rest of you, go get Melanie.' She paused. 'And the body.'

'The body?' Sean asked, aghast. 'You mean we have to bring it here?'

Faye gave him a shove. 'Where else do you suggest we revive it? Now go!'

Cassie went to where Diana was seated at the table while the others sprang into action.

'The diadem's hidden in my room,' Diana said solemnly. 'Should we go together?'

Cassie nodded. 'So it seems Faye's getting her way after all. She wanted to use the Tools, and now we are.'

Diana reached for her bag. 'You can still back out if you're not comfortable with this.'

'Are you comfortable with it?' Cassie asked.

'I want Constance to be alive,' Diana said. 'And once we're done with the spell, we'll put each relic right back in its hiding place.'

'But you said there could be repercussions.'

Diana remained still for a moment and then spoke with care. 'All magic has repercussions, Cassie. Power always comes with consequences.'

Then she turned away as if the statement was nothing and fished through her bag for her keys. 'Let's go get the Tools. I'll drive.'

Chapter Eight

The kitchen was shadowy and quiet when Cassie stepped inside. Her mother wasn't home, and she was glad. She didn't want to have to explain why she was hauling bricks out of the fireplace. Just up the block, Diana was retrieving the tiara and whatever other materials they'd need to complete the resuscitation spell. And a little farther down Crowhaven Road, the rest of the group was somehow going to convince Melanie to allow them to bring her great-aunt's body to the lighthouse. Before this year, Cassie had never even seen a real dead body, and now she was going to put her hands over one and try to bring it back to life.

The fireplace wasn't such a creative hiding spot for the bracelet, Cassie knew, but it had worked successfully for so many years, why try to think up someplace different?

Deep inside its gaping stone mouth, she found the silver document box just as she'd left it. And when she removed its ancient lid, the bracelet glistened inside, as if it were celebrating the sudden, surprising light.

Cassie allowed herself to admire the bracelet's beauty for only a second. She ran her fingers over the intricate design on its rich silver surface and felt its weight in her hands. But then Diana called to her from outside.

'Be right there!' she yelled, and ran upstairs to quickly change into her ceremonial white shift.

Once she was dressed and ready, she found Diana waiting for her on the front porch swing with a large cotton sack at her side. She'd also changed into her ceremonial shift, but there was a composure to Diana's appearance that Cassie could only aspire to. Even under all this stress, Diana remained in control.

Cassie reached for her hand, hoping some of the strength would rub off Diana's skin onto hers. And somehow it did. A few moments of holding Diana close calmed her.

'We're doing the right thing,' Diana said. 'We need Constance.'

Cassie remembered what a refuge Constance had been since she lost her grandmother. And all the afternoons she'd spent in her parlour, learning new spells and studying ancient rituals. Constance was the only connection to the old ways the Circle had.

'I know we are,' Cassie said in her most courageous voice. 'I'm ready to go.'

'Okay, everyone, let's get started.' Diana emptied the cotton sack onto the table when they arrived at the lighthouse and immediately began reading directions from her Book of Shadows.

It didn't surprise Cassie how everyone automatically turned to Diana in moments like this – moments when it really mattered. She would always be the most natural leader among them, no matter what.

'The body should be entirely covered in white cloth of two layers,' Diana read aloud to Adam. 'With head and face veiled in tulle.' She gestured to a pile of fine white netting on the table.

Adam nodded. 'I'll take care of it,' he said.

Nick, Chris and Doug pushed all the furniture to the room's perimeter. Melanie kneeled in the centre beside the covered body. Cassie helped Deborah drape the windows with purple linens.

Diana approached Faye carrying two golden censers. 'We have to fumigate the chamber with sage and frankincense,' she said.

Faye had changed into her ceremonial black shift and she was already wearing the green leather garter with its seven silver buckles. She accepted the censers from Diana and then called Sean over to tend to the chore. 'Where's the diadem?' she asked.

Diana nodded over to Melanie, sitting solemnly with the diadem on her head. 'She's the one who gets to wear the Tools tonight,' Diana said. 'She's doing the conjuring. The rest of us are her support.'

Even Faye couldn't disagree that Melanie should be the one leading this spell, but she still tore the garter from her leg with fury before walking it over to Melanie. Cassie followed close behind her, removing the bracelet from her wrist on her way.

In a few minutes, the room had been properly prepared and Diana called for the ritual to begin.

'Faye and Cassie, will you do the honours of casting the circle according to my instructions? Forgive me if I go slowly – this text is really hard to read – but I'll do my best. Is everyone ready?'

Cassie looked around the dimly lit room. She wasn't the only one who seemed nervous, but nobody was about to back out now. Melanie appeared to be in a cloudy-eyed daze, but she looked more beautiful wearing the Master Tools than Cassie had ever seen her.

Diana cleared her throat and began reading aloud. 'A magic circle is to be formed upon the ground with an ink of soot and port wine. A second circle is formed half a foot within the first.'

Together Cassie and Faye formed the circles around Melanie and Constance, using the chalice of ink Diana had prepared.

'And within there,' Diana continued, 'cast a triangle, the centre of which will serve as the resting place of the deceased and primary conjurer.'

Cassie and Faye formed the triangle within the circles, outlining Melanie and Constance.

'Everyone get inside,' Diana said. 'And then I'll close the outer circle with the four layers of protection.'

Quickly the group arranged itself, kneeling upon the outer circle's perimeter as Diana called on the elements.

'Powers of Air, protect us,' Diana called out. 'Powers of Fire, protect us.'

Cassie closed her eyes and listened.

'Powers of Water, protect us.' Diana enunciated each syllable with precision. 'And finally,' she said, 'I call on the powers of Earth to protect us.'

Diana then joined the circle beside Cassie and continued reading from her Book of Shadows. 'To commence, the conjurer must light a black candle and cast it over the body seven times thereon, calling the name of the spirit to be raised.'

All eyes turned to Melanie now. Cassie wondered if she had the strength to do it. But the Tools glistened and Melanie's posture straightened as she lit the candle and passed it over the white sheet, calling out, 'Great-Aunt Constance, Constance Burke, hear us.'

Diana continued, 'Then from a golden chalice of dried amaranth flowers, sprinkle the body and its surrounding area.'

While Melanie did the sprinkling, Diana said, 'Melanie, repeat after me: Thou who art mourned, see now the nature of this mourning.'

And Melanie repeated, 'Thou who art mourned, see now the nature of this mourning.'

Cassie felt her eyes fill with tears as Diana chanted:

> *This is the spell that we intone*
> *Flesh to flesh and bone to bone*
> *Sinew to sinew and vein to vein*
> *Constance shall be whole again*

They all concentrated hard, harnessing their powers together as one. Cassie could sense an energy rising up from the centre triangle, webbing out to each member of the group, linking them all together in a maze of light.

Diana read aloud, 'After a moment of silence and concentration, uncover the face of the deceased. Then call to the spirit again, affectionately. Say "Welcome."'

With quivering hands, Melanie gently unveiled Constance's face. 'Great-Aunt Constance,' she said. 'Welcome.'

'The body will stir,' Diana read. 'The eyes will open, and then the desired awakening.'

The room crackled with energy. Cassie could feel it zipping and twisting around her in spirals, but she wasn't afraid of it any more. The air around them warmed and Cassie could see the life flickering back into Constance's face slowly, like the rising sun.

Then a shape began to form. Cassie noticed it faintly at first in the glow on Constance's forehead, but then it grew bigger and brighter until it stood out like an iridescent bruise. It was most definitely a symbol, a primal-looking mark resembling two crooked *U*-shapes within a hexagon. Then everything went dark. The light that had come to Constance's face, the symbol, the candles illuminating the room – all of it disappeared, as if a heavy blanket were dropped from the ceiling, snuffing the room to death.

Diana lit her lantern and held it up to Melanie's grief-stricken face. Her great-aunt Constance was still dead. And now she had to experience her death all over again.

'The spell didn't work,' Laurel said.

'But it was working.' Diana's eyes frantically searched the group. 'Didn't you all feel it?'

'Yes, of course,' Adam said. 'I don't understand what went wrong.'

Faye was silent but looked just as confused as the others.

Adam spoke out again. 'Is there anything more to the spell, Diana? Does it say anything else in your book?'

Diana squinted at the bottom of the page she'd been reading, then turned to the next page, and then turned it back again.

'It's nearly illegible,' she said. 'But there's a scrawled line here at the bottom edge.' She held her lantern close to the book's tiny wording.

'It says, "Should nothing result, and this witch hath been true . . ." and then it stops. Whatever it said next got smudged out.'

'Smudged out?' Faye grabbed the book from Diana's hands to have a look for herself. 'How could something so important be smudged out?'

'It's a three-hundred-year-old book,' Adam said in Diana's defence. 'It's not that hard to believe.'

Cassie wondered if she was the only one who saw the symbol appear on Constance's forehead. Or had she imagined it? Over the echoes of Melanie's sobs, she knew it wasn't the right time to ask. Constance was lost to them forever.

It was late by the time Cassie got back home, but her mother was awake, lying on the sofa in her nightgown. She sat upright as soon as Cassie stepped in from outside. 'Are you all right?' she asked.

'Yes,' Cassie assured her, closing and locking the door behind her.

'How's Melanie?'

'She's been better.' Cassie pulled her jacket tightly closed, not wanting her mother to see she was wearing the white shift.

'And Constance?'

Cassie hesitated. She realised her mother was eyeing the Master bracelet on Cassie's left wrist. 'You know then,' Cassie said. 'About the resuscitation spell.'

Her mom nodded and gestured for Cassie to join her on the sofa. 'I just figured,' she said. 'Did it work?'

At first Cassie simply shook her head and took off her coat. But she wanted to be able to tell her mom everything, even about the symbol she saw illuminating Constance's forehead. And for once she did, without holding anything back for her mother's benefit.

Her mother surprised her by listening, really listening this time. She didn't change the subject or become so overwhelmed with fear that Cassie had to worry about her more than herself.

Until she mentioned the symbol she saw appear on Constance's forehead.

'The symbol,' Cassie said, 'looked like something primal. Like two bent *U*-shapes inside a hexagon.' Cassie noticed the alarmed look that flashed across her mother's face. 'What is it?'

Her mother shook her head. 'Not two *U*-shapes,' she said. 'One. A *W*.'

Cassie didn't understand what she was hearing.

'*W*, as in Witch,' her mother said.

Cassie was breathless. Her mother closed her eyes for a moment and when she reopened them they looked as grim as two black coals.

'I know what went wrong with the spell,' she said. 'There's a way a witch can be killed that can never be reversed. But there's only one kind of person who can do it.'

'Who?' Cassie asked. 'What kind of person?'

'A witch hunter,' her mother said.

Chapter Nine

Witch hunters go back as far as witches. Just as Cassie was descended from a long line of powerful ancestors, the witch hunters, too, had their lineage. That's what Cassie's mom told her as they walked down Crowhaven Road towards Melanie's house.

They walked side by side, her mother carrying a casserole dish and Cassie holding a few soothing herbs from the garden. Cassie felt her hair lifted by the salty wind coming off the ocean and she watched the trees fill with that same wind. The birds nesting within the trees began to sing and a strange sort of calm came over her.

'The symbol you saw on Constance's forehead was an ancient mark only a true hunter could make,' her mother said. 'Something must have brought them to New Salem.'

Cassie noticed the tiny crocus buds just beginning to

poke their heads up from the ground alongside the sidewalk. *Spring is still on its way*, she thought, *even as we're being hunted and killed*. 'I wish whatever brought them to New Salem would leave,' she said.

Melanie's house was so crowded when they arrived that they could barely get through the door. It appeared that everyone who'd been at the spring festival and seen Constance collapse had come now to pay their respects to the old woman. The first familiar face Cassie saw belonged to Sally Waltman. What was she doing here? Had she come with Portia? Were Portia's brothers, Jordan and Logan, here, too?

A million worst-case scenarios raced through Cassie's mind. Were they hoping to turn Constance's wake into a celebration? Jordan and Logan were longtime enemies of the Circle, and Cassie wouldn't put it past them to gloat publicly over the death of a witch. But when Sally met Cassie's eyes and approached her with an outstretched hand, she recognised that Sally had come alone, with only good intentions.

'I'm so sorry for your loss, and for Melanie's loss,' she said. She looked a little nervous to be there. She fidgeted with her dress and played with her rust-coloured hair.

'Thank you,' Cassie said hesitantly.

Sally continued, speaking almost directly to Cassie's hesitation. 'I know I don't belong here,' she said, 'and that your friends don't even like me, but Constance always greeted me warmly when I'd see her in town, and she was a nice lady, and I guess I just wanted to stop by to pay my respects.'

Sally took a breath and Cassie gently patted her on the back. It was true, the Circle didn't like Sally very much, and she and Cassie would probably never really be friends, but since last autumn when they'd overlooked their differences and worked together to get through Black John's hurricane, they'd had an understanding. Sally was the closest thing the group had to an Outsider ally, and that was nothing to take lightly.

'It was good of you to come,' Cassie said. 'Really. This was a nice gesture and I know Melanie appreciates it.'

That seemed to put Sally at ease. Her small, wiry body relaxed.

'Speaking of Melanie,' Cassie's mother said, 'we should probably go find her.'

'Of course,' Sally said, and Cassie and her mother elbowed through the crowd as politely as they could until they located Melanie.

The group had Melanie surrounded like an army of

black-clad secret-service agents. Most days Cassie forgot how intimidating the Circle could appear to others and how superior they looked compared to average kids their age. It wasn't only their genetics that set them apart; it was also their attitude. *But*, Cassie wondered, *don't they ever grow weary of striving to appear so infinitely strong to the outside world*? Sometimes vulnerability was appropriate, and this was one of those times.

Cassie locked eyes with Adam and dreamed for a moment that they could run away together, far away from all this. He didn't even know yet how bad all this actually was. None of the Circle did. How would they react when she told them everything she'd learned from her mother about witch hunters?

Cassie went to Adam first, just to breathe in his scent and feel his strong arms around her body. Then she offered her condolences and the soothing herbs to Melanie.

Diana tapped Cassie on the shoulder and pulled her in for a tight squeeze. Hugging Diana was like hugging daylight, and she was about as constant. Tall, magisterial Diana could always be relied upon. 'How are you doing?' she whispered into Cassie's ear.

But before Cassie had the chance to answer, Diana got distracted. Her attention turned to someone else who'd just walked in. 'Scarlett's here,' she said.

It was a surprise to see Scarlett making her way through the crowd, dressed conservatively in all black with her wild hair tamed into a neat ponytail.

As she meandered through the crowd, Cassie noticed people stepping aside to let her pass. *How weird*, Cassie thought, but then it occurred to her the reason why: All these strangers must have thought Scarlett was one of the group. She assumed the air of belonging right there with Melanie and the rest of the Circle, and so people believed she did.

But when she finally reached Cassie and the others, some of that confidence fell away. 'I know I don't really know any of you,' she said, looking down. 'But I wanted to say I was sorry.'

Diana scanned Scarlett up and down with her sharp green eyes and then said in a slightly artificial tone of voice, 'It was nice of you to come.'

'Yes, thank you,' Melanie said.

Like Sally, Scarlett didn't have to be there, but she'd gone out of her way to show her support to Melanie and the group. *Maybe*, Cassie thought, *if any good could come from this crisis, it would be the start of better relations with Outsiders.*

Adam stepped in to make small talk with Scarlett, giving Cassie the chance to grab Diana and lead her to a quiet corner. 'Gather the others,' Cassie said quietly. 'Melanie, too. I know why the resuscitation spell didn't work.'

Diana's eyes grew wide. She took a step back to size up Cassie's expression and then immediately began rounding up the group.

Constance's garage was filled with ancient junk and knick-knacks that may or may not have been authentic magical relics. Two stone swords rested on hooks in the wall, bronze jewellery boxes and dusty heirloom books were stacked high on drooping shelves, and multicoloured stuffed birds hung precariously from wire pitched to the ceiling. A claw-foot table sat in the centre of the room in front of a sagging green couch.

Melanie sat on the couch, but everyone else remained standing, spread out between piles of cardboard boxes. They waited silently for Cassie to begin.

Melanie was examining her, leaning forward, eager to hear what Cassie knew. There were dark circles beneath her usually alert eyes and all the life had escaped from her features. Cassie suddenly worried this news might be more than she could handle at the moment.

Cassie bought some time and tried to soften the blow by explaining, step by step, the conversation she'd had with her mother the night before. She paced herself, carefully building up to the description of the symbol she saw on Constance's forehead before everything went black during the resuscitation spell.

'Did any of you see it?' she asked.

Everyone shook their head.

'How do you know it wasn't just a hallucination?' Faye asked with a tinge of malice. 'Or your overactive imagination?'

'Because Cassie has the sight,' Diana said. 'Tell us, Cassie, what exactly did the symbol look like?'

'Well,' Cassie glanced quickly at Melanie before she spoke, 'I thought it looked like a hexagon with two bent-up *U*-shapes inside it. But my mother corrected me.'

'It was a *W*,' Melanie said, almost to herself. 'Great-Aunt Constance was killed by a witch hunter.'

The room shuddered.

'This is bad,' Melanie said, shaking her head. 'I've read about that symbol.'

Adam sat beside Melanie on the sofa. 'Do you think this means there's someone in town targeting us?'

Melanie nodded, too numb to cry. 'And not amateurs

85

like the Bainbridge family, either. These guys are the real thing. They're descendants of an ancient clan of hunters.'

Adam's jaw tightened and his eyes sharpened to an intense navy blue. 'The hunter could be anyone.'

'Or hunters,' Diana said. 'There could be more than one.'

Laurel sat down on the couch on the other side of Melanie and reached for her hand. 'We have to be careful.'

'That's right,' Adam said, jumping up to pace the room, nearly bumping his head on various hanging fowl as he marched back and forth. 'And we have to stick together. More than ever. Is that understood?' He stood still and eyed each member of the group individually.

Then his gaze rested on Faye.

To Cassie's surprise, Faye had no snide remarks this time. She simply nodded. But this out-of-character response worried Cassie more than if Faye had been her inappropriate, obnoxious self. If Faye was frightened, they were in serious trouble.

Diana glanced at the door. The people inside the house were getting louder, and one muffled voice was asking for Melanie.

'I have to get back inside,' Melanie said.

Diana nodded. 'You should. Melanie, I'm sorry to leave, but I'm going to run home. I know I've seen a protection spell in my Book of Shadows somewhere. I'll look into it and see what I can do.'

'That's a good idea,' Melanie said, standing now but still holding on to Laurel's hand.

Hesitantly, they all began filing out of the garage, but Nick hung back, and Cassie took advantage of the opportunity to talk to him alone. She reached for his arm and started talking before he could say anything.

'I know you've been avoiding the group because of me,' she said. 'And I want you to stop doing that.'

Nick turned away, but she forced him to look at her. 'Listen to me. We have to stay close now. We're in serious danger.'

He squinted his mahogany eyes at her as if she were a foreign object.

'I don't want to see you get hurt,' Cassie said desperately. 'Please.'

'Well, thank you for your concern.' He said it sharply, like it was intended to cut her, but Nick always resorted to sarcasm when he started to feel something. It meant she'd gotten through to him, at least a little bit. She'd take what she could get for now.

Chapter Ten

Cassie woke up to sunlight streaming in her windows. Her room was bright but cold, and the March morning air contained a windy chill that shook the windows. She would have given anything to stay beneath her warm covers and hide from the day, but she knew that wasn't an option. Instead she got up, wrapped herself in her blue terrycloth bathrobe and made her way outside to fetch the newspaper. She assumed there would be a write-up on Constance in the obituary section.

There was no paper on the front porch, but Cassie did find Adam, curled up beneath his jacket, asleep on the porch swing. She watched him for a moment. How peaceful he looked, but he couldn't be comfortable. His long legs and arms were pretzelled into the swing, hanging halfway off. He'd probably been there all night.

This boy really loves me, Cassie thought to herself, looking down on his beautifully sculpted body, crunched as it was within the confines of the swing. *He probably loves me way too much.*

She reached out and grazed his cheekbone with her fingertips.

He smiled sleepily at her, stretching.

'What in the world are you doing out here?' she asked.

Adam quickly took inventory of his surroundings and rubbed the back of his sore neck. 'Protecting you.'

'From the witch hunters?' Cassie blurted out. 'But who was protecting you while you were out here all night protecting me?'

'I was,' Adam said, and then laughed. 'But I guess I dozed off.'

Cassie took his face into her hands. 'What am I going to do with you?' She kissed his chapped lips slowly and warmly. 'Promise me next time you'll at least come inside and sleep on the couch.'

Adam kissed her back passionately. He wrapped his strong arms around her and pulled her in close. She could smell the ocean on his clothes and in the creases of his neck. She kissed him there and expected to taste salt, but instead it tasted fresh and cold like ice.

'I promise,' he said with a shiver.

'Will you come inside now and let me warm you up?' she asked flirtatiously.

He blinked his long dark lashes at her and eagerly followed her through the door.

'Where's Faye?' Diana asked, but nobody seemed to know.

Diana had found a protective spell in her Book of Shadows, and she wanted to cast it upon the group as soon as possible. But they'd been waiting at the beach for over an hour.

'Faye's been late to every meeting this week,' Diana said. 'This is unacceptable. Suzan, will you call her again?'

'She's not answering,' Suzan said. 'She's been totally sketchy lately.'

Sean nodded. 'We had plans with her last night and she blew us out.'

If it were anyone other than Faye they were talking about, Cassie would have been worried. But she knew Faye would show up eventually. In the meantime, Cassie was glad to be at the beach rather than the lighthouse. She felt safe there among the long stretch of sand, the steady repetition of crashing waves, and the vast, limitless sky. She wanted to enjoy every last second they had before tourist season littered the sand with strangers. She imagined it now like a nightmare: foldout chairs as far as the eye could see, bratty sunbathers and self-righteous surfers; toppled-over soda cans and screaming, orange-fingered, Dorito-munching children. She much preferred a cold, abandoned beach to a hot, crowded one.

She thought of Scarlett then, how it would be nice to invite her out to the beach one night this week. Maybe they could build a bonfire and make s'mores. It would be a fun way to offset all this stressful Circle business.

Then Faye appeared, waking Cassie from her daydream. 'Am I late?' she said. 'Sorry.'

'Where have you been?' Diana asked.

'Trust me, you couldn't handle it.'

Diana ignored her comment. 'We need to begin the protection spell before the sun starts to set.'

Cassie tried to assume the role of a leader as the group arranged themselves into a wide circle formation. Diana knelt in front of a stone kettle, mixing together a dark, oily concoction.

'In this cauldron is salt water from the ocean mixed with blueberry oil and eucalyptus,' she said. Then she looked up at Faye and Cassie. 'Will the two of you, together, use the dagger to draw our circle around me?'

Faye unsheathed the silver dagger, which had been concealed beneath her flowing black skirt, strapped to the inside of her thigh. Her eyes narrowed, as they always did when she had a sharp object in her grasp.

'Give me your hand,' she said to Cassie. She guided Cassie's thin fingers around the dagger's pearl handle and enveloped them with her own. Together, as one, they drew the circle in the sand.

Each member of the group stepped inside as Melanie placed two candles on either end of the cauldron Diana was mixing.

'Here I place two candles,' Melanie announced according to ceremony. 'One blue, for physical protection, and one purple, for power and wisdom.'

As she bent down to light the candles, she recited a chant from Diana's Book of Shadows: 'Divine Goddess, God Divine, if evil dwells within this place, make it now leave our space.' She then positioned the book on the ground beside Diana and took her spot within the circle next to Laurel.

Diana stood in the centre of the circle holding up the cauldron. 'In order for this to work,' she said, 'you all need to picture a white light around you. Let it surround your whole body as I recite the chant.'

Everyone agreed and closed their eyes. Diana raised the cauldron high up to the sky and said, 'By the power of the Source, no evil shall enter here.'

Then Cassie closed her eyes, too, and pictured a white light wrapping itself around her like a warm winter coat. Diana's voice dropped an octave, and the chant left her throat like thunder.

> *Psychic hunters in the night*
> *Psychic hunters of the day*
> *Destroy no more what I achieve*
> *Destroy no more what I receive*

There were a few seconds of quiet, hindered only by the billowing wind and crashing waves. Then, Cassie heard the bell-like echo of Diana stirring the mixture inside the stone cauldron.

Diana continued.

> *With this potion, I anoint this Circle*
> *To be protected from you, this magic I do*

Cassie opened her eyes and watched Diana rub a smudge of the inky blue mixture upon her forehead with her thumb. Then she did the same to Faye's forehead, and Cassie's, and all the others.

When she finished anointing the group, Diana asked Cassie and Faye to join her in the centre. The three of them held hands around the cauldron and candles, with closed eyes. Cassie pictured the white light surrounding not only her own body now but the whole group as one. She imagined it encapsulating them like a giant helium balloon and floating them up to the safety of the cloudless sky.

Diana finished the spell.

By the power of this ocean, wide and deep,
By the power of day, and night, and powers three,
This is our will, so let it be!

Little by little, everyone opened their eyes.

'Did it work?' Sean asked, raising his fingers up to the blue smudge on his forehead.

'How long do we have to walk around with this oil on us?' Suzan asked. 'It probably causes breakouts.'

'We can go wash it off in the ocean in just a minute,' Diana said.

'So that's it?' Faye asked, picking up the dagger from

the sand and re-sheathing it beneath her skirt. 'We're invincible now? Why didn't we do this long ago?'

'There are conditions,' Diana said.

'What *conditions*?' Faye asked, mocking Diana's measured, proper tone of voice.

Diana wasn't bothered by Faye's ridicule, probably because she was so accustomed to it. 'We'll be safe from bodily harm inflicted by the hunters,' she said. 'But the spell only protects us on the island of New Salem. If we step beyond that, we're vulnerable.'

'So nobody leaves the island,' Adam said. 'Under any circumstances.'

He glanced over at Nick, who had taken to disappearing for days at a time, but Nick ignored him.

Diana dug a deep hole in the sand to discard the remaining potion. 'It also doesn't mean the hunters can't find us. So everyone has to be extra careful. We have to do everything we can to remain undetected.'

She stood up, wiped the sand from her hands and looked directly at Faye. 'We can't practise magic at all. The hunters will be looking for anything out of the ordinary to find out who we are.'

'What?' Faye charged at Diana like she might tackle her to the ground. 'Our magic is the only power we have.

How else are we supposed to defeat these guys if we can't use magic?'

Diana squared her thin shoulders to Faye and matched her gaze with equal ferocity. 'We find them before they find us,' she said. 'That's how we're going to defeat them.'

'Faye,' Melanie said, stepping between her and Diana, 'these are my aunt's murderers we're talking about. You're going to put your magic on hold, because if you don't, you're putting the whole group at risk. And we can't have that.'

Cool-headed Melanie had never threatened anyone in her life, but here she was, an inch taller than Faye, ready for a fight.

Adam got between them before things had a chance to escalate. 'Everyone needs to take a deep breath and calm down,' he said. 'We can't afford to be fighting each other right now.'

'No,' Melanie argued, shoving Adam's peacekeeping hand aside. 'What we can't afford is Faye not following Circle rules when our lives are at stake.'

'Please, Faye.' Adam was practically begging her to cooperate. 'No magic. Just until we figure out who the hunters are. Okay?'

'Fine. My God, you people are so boring.' Faye began

walking away, towards the ocean.

'That's not all,' Diana called out. 'We also need to be on the lookout for Outsiders who are getting too close. And anyone new in town.'

Diana glanced sharply at Cassie. She didn't name Scarlett specifically, but she didn't have to. Then she turned to Faye. 'So you need to lay off Max.'

Suzan smirked. 'How can she lay off him when he won't even let her lay on him?'

Faye looked like all the fight had been knocked out of her. It obviously bothered her that Max wasn't falling under her spell like every other boy in school.

'Is *that* all?' she asked Diana.

Diana nodded. 'For now.'

Faye turned and marched towards the ocean to wash her forehead clean. Her black skirt and hair flowed behind her like a dark shadow.

The next morning at school, Faye pulled into the empty parking space beside Cassie and Adam. 'Is Diana here yet?' she asked, before she was even out of the car.

'Not yet,' Adam said. 'What's wrong?'

Faye looked anxiously around the school lot, at Sally and Portia gathering their pompoms and books, at a few lacrosse players playing catch, and finally at Suzan sitting on the hood of her Corolla, applying mascara.

'I can't handle this no-magic thing,' Faye said. 'I had to wait for water to boil this morning. Can you believe that? Eight minutes. Like I have nothing better to do with my time.'

'I'm with Faye,' Suzan said from behind her hand mirror. 'I feel so ordinary, so unexceptional. It's dehumanising.'

'And on top of all that, you have a stain on your shirt,' Faye said.

'I know.' Suzan scratched at the blotch on her collar. 'How do normal people get ketchup out of their clothes?'

Diana zipped her Volvo into the spot next to Faye and hurriedly pushed her door open. She was less put together than usual. Her hair was loose and wild, and her jacket was hanging half off. She had a coffee cup in one hand and a bagel in the other, which she shoved in her mouth to dig for her books in the back seat.

'See,' Faye said. 'Even Diana's a mess. We can't live like this.'

Until this moment, Cassie hadn't realised how much her friends used magic in their everyday lives.

Adam helped Diana with her books. 'This isn't easy

for any of us,' he said. 'But we have to stick with it. It's only temporary.'

The rest of the group arrived sporadically. Whether it was purely psychological or not, Cassie noticed they all seemed a bit distressed without their magic – except Deborah, who tore through the parking lot with her motorcycle up on one wheel. Cars and people scattered from her path until she lowered the front tyre down, screeched to a halt and cut the engine.

'Where's your helmet?' Diana asked, once Deborah joined the rest of the group.

Deborah rolled her eyes. 'I'm not going to mess up my hair with a helmet when I'm invincible.'

'You may be invincible,' Diana said. 'But you can still accidentally run over somebody else.'

'Then maybe *they* should be wearing helmets,' Faye said, which drew a sharp look from Diana.

'Please, don't abuse the protection spell,' Diana said. 'It's not an excuse to be irresponsible.'

'You're telling me this?' Deborah removed one of her leather gloves, then the other and pointed at the sky. 'What about them?'

Cassie noticed everyone in the parking lot had stopped going about their business and were focused on something overhead. She followed the communal gaze, just as Diana did, to find Chris and Doug on the roof of the school building.

Someone screamed out, 'What are those maniacs doing up there?'

'I think they're fencing,' another voice said.

Diana had to look away. 'Please tell me they didn't bring real swords to school.'

'Technically they're not *in* school,' Sean said. 'They're *on* it.'

Chris and Doug sparred back and forth, swinging wildly at each other, ducking and bobbing. The crowd gasped as Doug took a slicing hit on the shoulder. He cried out, dropped to the ground and fake blood spurted from the rooftop like a sprinkler. Their schoolmates started to scream, but then Doug jumped back to his feet with one arm hidden within his sleeve and resumed the fight.

'They're having way too much fun with this,' Adam said.

Cassie eyed the crowd of spectators, wondering if any of them noticed Chris and Doug were impenetrable to the swords' sharp blades. But everyone was so accustomed to the twins' crazy antics that none of them seemed to question it.

Even Max, who was still the talk of the school, was amused by their performance. He was standing with his lacrosse friends and the swarm of pretty girls who fluttered around him at all times. The girls had, for once, diverted their attention away from Max to watch the rooftop.

Doug slashed Chris across the chest, slitting his shirt diagonally open. It flapped like a flag in the wind. 'Serves you right, brother,' Chris called out. 'This T-shirt was one of yours.'

Laughter passed over the crowd in a wave. Max shook his head, stepped away from his crew, and made his way over to Diana.

'Someone should stop those two,' he said. 'Before they're both completely naked.'

Cassie observed how Max's admirers visibly sighed at the sight of him talking to Diana. They obviously considered her competition.

'But I can't be the one to stop them,' Max continued, leaning in close to her. 'Can't you work some of your magic?'

Diana froze for a second, but it was clear to Cassie that Max meant nothing by it. He was fixated on Diana's eyes.

'You must have every guy in school at your beck and

call,' he said to her. 'I imagine if anyone can get them down, it's you.'

Diana exhaled deeply and laughed. She self-consciously tried to smooth her hair down, but it remained beautifully tousled. 'If only that were true,' she said.

'I can get them off the roof,' Faye offered, but Max ignored her.

'It's just that if my dad catches them up there, there's no telling what he'll do,' Max said. 'He's not big on kids bringing weapons to school.'

'Understandably,' Diana answered, nodding. But before she could return her attention to Chris and Doug, Nick appeared on the roof behind them.

'The show's over,' he called out, approaching the two of them like he might wring their necks.

Chris and Doug looked at each other and dropped their swords. They raised their hands in defence and backed away from Nick, edging closer and closer to the roof's edge. The crowd fell silent. It had to be a twenty-foot drop.

Nick caught on to the trick and stood still. 'That's enough,' he said. 'You had your fun. Now just come down quietly.'

Chris and Doug glanced at the crowd and then latched

hands. 'Never!' they screamed, and leaped from the roof, landing on a large dumpster below.

People covered their mouths and turned away. Even Max winced, subtly turning his face in towards Diana's as he did so. But the twins landed with a synchronised tumble. Without a scratch, they climbed down and took their bows.

Chapter Eleven

Cassie was in town running errands when the rich aroma of the Witch's Brew Coffee Shop filled her lungs. *Coffee*, she thought. What a good idea. The Witch's Brew was a gimmick, plain and simple, capitalising on the town's Salem witch trial-related history. At night it featured strobe lights and white cotton cobwebs, and was a favourite place for anyone from out of town looking for an overpriced drink with a gothic name. The locals, and Cassie's friends especially, avoided the place for obvious reasons. But in the light of day, the Brew could almost pass as an ordinary coffee shop, and they'd just set up their outdoor tables. Cassie figured it wouldn't be so bad if she could sit outside sipping her drink in the sun, so she looked for an empty seat.

That was when she noticed that familiar dyed red hair

she knew belonged to Scarlett. She was bent over a book, reading and mindlessly chewing on a pencil. Cassie's first instinct was to go sit with her, but then she remembered the new rule. Outsiders were off limits for now.

It wasn't fair. The Circle shouldn't be able to dictate whom Cassie had coffee with. But even Faye was willing to relinquish some of her personal freedom for the good of the group. And Cassie had to get to the lighthouse anyway. In lieu of being able to do magic, Melanie and Laurel were resorting to herbology to pass the time. They'd asked Cassie to bring over the flowers from a rare herb in her garden – the Plymouth gentian. Cassie felt for the paper bag containing the flowers in her tote, as if to remind herself of the errand's importance. She turned to go just as Scarlett noticed her.

'Cassie?' Scarlett's face instantly lit up. 'It's so good to see you,' she said. 'Come sit with me.'

'I can't,' Cassie said, scanning the surrounding area. 'I only have a minute.'

'Sit for only a minute then.' Scarlett closed her book and pushed it aside.

Scarlett looked so lonely sitting there by herself. It would have been cruel to decline.

'What are your plans for today?' Cassie asked casually.

Scarlett raised her hands and looked left and right. 'This,' she said. 'It ain't much.'

Cassie offered her a polite chuckle. 'Thanks again for coming to Melanie's the other day. I'm sorry I kind of lost track of you and didn't get to say goodbye.'

Scarlett's dark eyes radiated affection. 'No problem,' she said. Then she took a long sip of her iced coffee and seemed to be weighing something in her mind or trying to figure something out.

Cassie felt like she was being examined so deeply that Scarlett could have been counting each of her pores or every one of her eyelashes, but Cassie just let her. For some reason, it didn't make her feel self-conscious. She didn't know why, but she wanted Scarlett to know her, and to really see her.

After another moment passed, Scarlett said, 'I really like your friends. And since I don't know anyone on the island, I was hoping to make a good impression.'

Cassie knew this was the moment where, if she were a regular girl without a Circle to answer to, she would ask Scarlett to hang out. Instead, she offered her a pathetic-sounding conciliation. 'I was the new kid not long ago,' Cassie said. 'And I know how brutal making friends in this town can be.'

Scarlett's full red lips broke into a wide smile. 'That's why I'm going to guilt you into being friends with me.'

Cassie laughed. She enjoyed Scarlett's unpretentiousness. She was just the kind of no-nonsense girl Cassie would have been friends with back in California.

'For example,' Scarlett said, 'I'm going to remind you that I moved here with a single pathetic suitcase to convince you to go shopping with me.'

Cassie remembered Diana's snarky comment about Scarlett's suitcase and was embarrassed by it all over again. She glanced at her watch. She had another two hours before she had to be at the lighthouse. What could be the harm in going around to a few stores for an hour?

'Lucky for you, shopping is one of my favourite leisure-time activities,' Cassie said.

'Does that mean you're in?' Scarlett asked.

'Why not?' Cassie stood up. 'My errands can wait.'

Scarlett shot out of her seat. 'That worked even better than I thought it would.'

Shopping with Scarlett was the perfect diversion from all of Cassie's troubles. Since she couldn't talk about any of the Circle's issues, she had to put them out of her mind entirely. It was like getting to be somebody else for a few hours, somebody with normal concerns. Concerns like, *Is forty dollars too much to pay for a tank top even if it's really really soft?* And Scarlett was a master shopper; she could pluck out the best item on a sale rack with the speedy foresight even a witch could admire. She somehow talked Cassie into buying turquoise-blue feathered earrings.

'These are more your style than mine,' Cassie said, just after the impulse buy.

'We can share them.' Scarlett smiled brightly. 'In fact, we can share most of this stuff. That's the beauty of being the same size.'

Cassie agreed and then suggested they unload their shopping bags into the trunk of her car before searching out the perfect summer shoes. She and Scarlett slipped so easily into friendship that Cassie forgot she was supposed to be keeping her distance from her. So the sight of Diana stepping out of her Volvo across the parking lot didn't strike Cassie as an immediate cause for alarm. Her panic didn't set in until Diana's eyes met hers – first with the delight of a surprise encounter, followed by a narrowing, painful displeasure. Cassie had been caught blatantly defying a promise she had made to the Circle.

Diana approached them gradually. Her 'Hello' sounded

more like a snub than a greeting. 'I see you two have been having a good time,' she said, gesturing to their shopping bags.

Scarlett, sensing the coldness in Diana's voice, smiled politely but said nothing.

'I ran into Scarlett unexpectedly,' Cassie said.

Diana derided Cassie with her eyes. 'I guess there's a lot of that happening today.'

Cassie bit her lip but said nothing.

Scarlett shifted uncomfortably and said, 'Maybe I should get going.'

'No,' Diana said. 'I should.' She stepped past them towards the mall's entrance. 'I'll talk to you later, Cassie.'

'That girl really does not like me,' Scarlett said, once Diana was out of earshot.

Cassie wasn't sure how to begin defending Diana's behaviour. It's not like Scarlett could possibly understand. 'It has nothing to do with you,' Cassie said. 'Believe me. But I'm still sorry.'

Scarlett shrugged it off. 'I'll let you make it up to me by joining me for dinner.'

Cassie was torn. She knew the right thing to do was to separate from Scarlett and immediately go do damage control with Diana, but she'd been having such a good time, and breaking off from Scarlett now would only hurt her feelings.

'How about burgers from Buffalo House?' Scarlett asked. 'I'm buying.'

'I really shouldn't.' Cassie felt for the bag of herbs in her tote and looked at her watch. But a bacon cheeseburger sounded like bliss right now. A girl had to eat, right?

'Okay,' Cassie said at last. 'If you come with me to run this errand first. It's just a quick favour for a friend. Then we can go for burgers.'

Scarlett beamed. 'Perfect,' she said.

Of course, the Circle would not approve of Cassie bringing Scarlett along, but she was careful. And Scarlett didn't ask any questions, even when Cassie insisted she stay in the car while she ran into the abandoned lighthouse with a paper sack under her arm. And since Melanie and Laurel hadn't arrived yet, all she had to do was drop the bag onto the table and go. It took less than a minute to get in and out. And then she and Scarlett were free to race over to Buffalo House for burgers.

Later that night, Adam came over to Cassie's for a cozy night of popcorn and a movie. Her mom was upstairs, allowing them their privacy in the den, where they lounged on the soft-backed couch. Cassie sunk down into the cushion with her head resting on Adam's shoulder, breathing him in. She could get drunk off the smell of him. They weren't really watching the movie, or at least Cassie wasn't. She had her eyes closed and was focused on Adam's gentle caresses, how he slid his soft fingers up the inside of her arm, starting at the wrist, moving to the elbow, and back down again. She could have done that all night; the movie was just noise in the background. But then Adam looked down to see if she was awake.

'You're sleeping,' he said.

Cassie opened her eyes. 'I'm not sleeping, just enjoying.'

Adam got a serious look in his eye and Cassie was sure he was about to lean in to kiss her. This was how their movie-watching usually turned out. But this time, instead of kissing her, he clicked the movie off and sat upright.

'There's something I've been meaning to talk to you about,' he said.

Cassie also sat up straight and pulled her knees into her chest. She couldn't imagine what was about to come out of his mouth. A million possibilities, one worse than the next, raced through her mind.

'Diana said she saw you out shopping this afternoon,' Adam said. 'With Scarlett.'

Cassie stiffened. 'Oh.'

'She thinks your friendship with Scarlett is getting too close.'

'Well, thank you for telling me what Diana thinks,' Cassie said.

The remark made Adam raise his voice, which was something he never did in Cassie's presence. 'I don't think I should have to tell you that you're putting yourself at risk by spending so much time with an Outsider,' he said. 'You're putting all of us at risk.'

'Is that even how you really feel, or is that how Diana feels?'

Adam jerked back as if Cassie had taken a swing at him. 'What's that supposed to mean?'

'Why are you siding with Diana on this? You've always been the one to jump to the defence of Outsiders.'

'Cassie, what's going on with you? Come here.' Adam tried to reach for her, but she pulled away.

Cassie knew she was overreacting – this was Adam, the guy who stayed up all night on her front porch just to protect her. And Adam and Diana had been friends their whole lives; of course Diana went to him for advice. But she still didn't want him to touch her.

'I'm not siding with anyone,' Adam said. 'These aren't normal circumstances. You know that.'

But all Cassie could hear right now was Diana in Adam's words, and she couldn't help but be a little hurt.

'I feel with my entire being that Scarlett is safe,' Cassie said.

Adam looked like he was about to reach for Cassie again, but then he thought better of it. 'I just want you to be careful,' he said. 'I'm always on your side. You know that.'

He carefully moved in closer to her. 'I'm sorry I raised my voice. But I feel strongly about this. We have no way of knowing that Scarlett isn't a witch hunter. She arrived in town the same night Constance died.'

'You're being ridiculous,' Cassie said.

'No, you're being ridiculous. And stubborn.'

Cassie took a deep breath and tried to settle down. 'Let's just drop it, okay?'

But Adam refused. 'I know you really like Scarlett,' he said. 'And I get it, I do. She seems nice and funny and pretty. We all like her, but it's not a good time to let your guard down.'

'It never is when you're one of us.'

'You say that like you don't want to be one of us, like it's some kind of curse.'

'Let's just finish the movie,' Cassie said.

'Cassie, look at me.'

'I'll stop hanging out with her, okay?' Cassie shouted. 'I ran into her by accident, but I'm sure Diana didn't mention that part.'

Cassie clicked the TV back on. She stared straight ahead and sat as far away from Adam as the couch would allow. She was done talking for the night.

Chapter Twelve

Cassie slept late into the afternoon the next day, which was unlike her. Normally she was an early riser, whether she wanted to be or not. But she must have needed the rest, because she woke up feeling refreshed and with a clearer head than she had the night before. Cassie's argument with Adam had left her feeling confused and upset last night, but today was a new day. And it was beautiful and sunny, not a cloud in the sky.

After getting dressed in her most comfortable jeans and favourite blue sweater, Cassie decided to head out for a walk. She wasn't quite ready yet to talk to Adam, or anyone really, but hopefully while she walked, the words would start coming to her, and she'd return home knowing just what to say to make everything right again. What Cassie needed was to better understand her own feelings. She wasn't a jealous person, and she didn't want to be. But she also couldn't ignore what was bothering her about Adam and Diana. She owed it to both of them, and to herself, to be honest. She knew they had a history together that she couldn't compete with.

Cassie tied her sneakers tightly and went out the back door. She trudged through the maze of her grandmother's herb garden and across the surrounding acre of swaying green grass. She stepped over a few soggy piles of stray leaves and along the path of sand and dirt that led to the bluff.

There she found Nick out by the water's edge. He'd taken his leather jacket off and tossed it on the ground beside him. The wind off the water was blowing through his white T-shirt as if he were flying. It fanned his dark-brown hair up from his sober face. Watching Nick when he didn't have his defences up was like overhearing a secret. It made Cassie feel special to witness it but also a little bit guilty.

Cassie had wanted to be alone, but now she wanted nothing more than to be with Nick. Not in a romantic sense, of course. She loved Adam, but that didn't mean she and Nick couldn't be friends. So she went to him, preparing herself the whole way for his rejection of her company. But she felt she had to try at least. Nick may have been dark and brooding, he may have been unpredictable, and most days he could even be called rude – but there was a solid centre beneath all that, and it was pure, like the crystalline core to a rough rock. Cassie had seen it, and she was determined to break through his tough exterior to reach it again. She missed his friendship – even though she knew she was pushing him to be friends when their break-up was still so fresh.

'Hi,' she called out to him from a few steps back, not wanting to startle him.

He turned slowly, unsurprised to see her, almost like he was expecting her.

'Hi,' he said, which was invitation enough for Cassie to join him.

'How are you?' Cassie asked.

'Okay. How are you?'

'Good.'

It was awkward, definitely, but as they persevered through it, they began to slowly settle into their old habits. Nick teased her, pretending to be cruel, and Cassie rolled with his punches, laughing too loud. She'd wanted this for so long, she didn't want to mess it up, but there was one thing she couldn't let go.

'Can I ask you something?' she said, when there was a lull in their conversation.

Nick nodded, his jaw strong. 'You can ask me anything, but it doesn't mean I'll answer you.'

Cassie grinned. 'Did you come out here hoping to see me?'

'Wow, you're conceited.' Nick cracked up laughing.

'Is that a yes?'

Nick stopped laughing then and just smiled. He was so stingy with his full-toothed smile, Cassie had forgotten how beautiful and bright it was when it happened. Its scarcity only made it that much more valuable.

'Maybe the thought of you coming out here vaguely crossed my mind,' Nick said. 'I have missed this between us.'

At last. This was the Nick she knew.

'Me too,' Cassie said.

'Now I get to ask you something.' Nick flashed his bad-boy grin. 'Is Adam driving you crazy yet?'

'Nick!'

'He is. I know he is. Don't even try to deny it.'

'No comment,' Cassie said, laughing. But then she added, 'I guess I'm still getting used to his—'

'Smothering?'

'His goodness,' Cassie scolded. 'Now be nice.'

Nick suddenly appeared lighter, happier. Maybe all he needed to feel better was to take a good shot at Adam.

Cassie let her eyes go soft on the ocean. 'I promise things will go back to normal,' she said. 'For you and me. For all of us.'

But the moment those words left her lips, dark clouds formed overhead, too fast to be natural. They were ominous clouds of the sort you'd see in movies about the apocalypse. Nick grabbed Cassie's hand and they took a few cautious steps back, away from the ocean.

'What's happening?' Cassie asked. 'Is it a tornado? Do you even get those around here?'

'I don't know what this is.' Nick scanned the surrounding area for a safe shelter. 'We have to get out of here. All these trees. We have to try to run to your house.'

They started running, but they only made it a few steps when streaks of furious lightning began flashing all around them, seemingly right at them.

'Keep running,' Nick screamed, 'and cover your head.'

Ice-cold rain poured down, pelting them like needle-pointed arrows. The sky was completely black except for the lightning, which, when it flashed, illuminated the angry wind in the trees. The blustering sand and litter stirred up from the ground. Cassie strived to keep her eyes closed to the debris but also open enough to follow Nick's course of escape.

'We'll never make it,' Cassie screamed breathlessly. 'We should try a spell, to stop it.'

'No!' Nick yelled. 'No magic. Keep running.'

One flash after the next, the lightning and thunder reminded Cassie of fireworks.

'It's them, isn't it?' Cassie cried out. 'The hunters.'

Nick stopped running for a second and Cassie also stopped, breathing heavily. Nick's thick neck was pulsing; his chest was heaving. 'I think so,' he said. 'It could be a trick to get us to use our magic.'

Then a lightning bolt struck a willing target – one of the many elm trees nearby. It cracked and sparked from the blow.

Cassie shielded her eyes with her hand like a visor, watching the elm shiver and smoke. 'Seems like they might already know we're witches, don't you think?'

Then another tree right beside that one was hit, and then another, each one closer to Cassie and Nick than the one before. Finally, a fiery bolt crashed at the ground right next to Cassie's feet. She screamed and Nick pushed her out of the way, shielding her body with his own.

Cassie and Nick were both on the ground now, she beneath him. His broad muscular body was heavy on hers.

'Are you okay?' he asked. Rainwater dripped from his face onto hers.

'Yes,' Cassie said. From beneath him she watched the trees that had been hit succumb to wild orange flames. It was the most furious fire Cassie had ever seen, with billowing black smoke rising up from it like a ghost.

That could have been me, Cassie thought to herself. If Nick hadn't thrown her out of the way, she would have been dead.

It was a sight to see, those once great elms darken and wither to ash so fluidly. Their rugged brown bark melted at the will of the heat, like a chocolate bar left out in the sun.

Whatever the hunters were trying to prove, they'd proven it. Clearly they were powerful and they were willing to kill. They weren't witches, but this kind of control over the elements looked like black magic to Cassie. What kind of witch hunters used the same tactics as evil witches?

'They're so close,' Cassie said.

Nick let some of his weight off Cassie's quivering body beneath him. 'And they're getting closer every minute.'

It seemed to Cassie like there was no escape. She and Nick could get up and keep running, but the lightning and thunder would follow their every step until it finally hit its bullseye, striking them down with a ball of fire that would burn and bend their bones like the brittle branches of an old elm tree. Or they could lie right there on the ground, unmoving, clutching each other and closing their eyes to it all. They could go with it easily, rather than try to fight it. Dying side by side with Nick was better than being shot down from the sky.

And then as if it had all been a dream, the rain suddenly came to a halt, the lightning stopped and the sky cleared the way for the sun. The day returned, eerily and beautifully, to the perfect colour photograph it had been before. If the trees at their side hadn't still been steadily burning, clouding the air around them with bleak black smoke, Cassie would have believed she'd imagined the whole nightmarish scene.

'I guess we passed the test,' Nick said, standing up and brushing off his jeans. He ran his fingers through his soaking-wet hair and then offered Cassie his broad hand to help her to her feet.

'How is that?' Cassie asked, taking Nick's hand. 'By not dying?'

'It's a pretty good start.' Nick put his sturdy arm around Cassie's drenched sweater. 'Let's get you home.'

Cassie looked up into his mahogany eyes gratefully. She'd never forget the way he'd protected her. Without a moment's hesitation, he was willing to die for her.

'I'm only going home if you're coming with me,' she said.

'Well, I'm sure as heck not staying out here,' Nick said playfully, trying to make light of the situation.

'Nick.' Cassie refused to take another step until he looked her in the eyes and acknowledged what had just passed between them.

'What?'

'Thank you,' she said.

He shook his head and looked away again. 'You don't have to thank me.'

'Yes, I do.'

Nick started to laugh awkwardly, nervously. The kind of laugh that comes out when you're trying not to cry. Then he pulled Cassie in towards him and kissed her affectionately on the forehead, like a big brother might do. 'No problem,' he said.

Chapter Thirteen

Cassie and Nick heard fire trucks in the distance as they walked towards Cassie's house. To extinguish the burning trees, Cassie figured. They sped up their pace to be safely out of the line of suspicion for arson. There was no telling what angle the hunters would take in order to destroy them.

Once they were safely shut into Cassie's house, Nick went into overdrive. 'We should tell the others,' he said. 'We should get them all over here right now.'

His clothes were soaked through from the rain and his hair dripped down in front of his face.

'Wait,' Cassie said, moving from the kitchen to the living room. 'There's time for that.' She retrieved two large bath towels from the linen closet and tossed one at Nick. 'Dry yourself off,' she said.

He laughed. 'I guess we are a little wet.' In one swift motion, he pulled his T-shirt over his head and wrung it out over the kitchen sink.

Cassie caught herself gaping at his muscular torso and quickly turned away. 'I'm going to go change,' she said, running off to her bedroom. 'I'll be right back.'

When she returned, Nick appeared mostly dry and his shirt was thankfully back on. But so were his shoes, and Cassie knew Nick was about to bolt.

'You know what?' Nick said, moving towards the door. 'I'm going to go home and take a hot shower. Then I'll let the others know what happened.'

As much as Cassie wanted Nick to stay there with her, she knew she had to let him go. 'A hot shower does sound nice,' she said.

Nick paused with his hand on the doorknob. 'I assume you'll take care of telling Adam.'

Cassie nodded. But once Nick was gone, all she could do was sink into the couch.

She lost track of how long she was sitting there, but it was long enough that when her mother came home, she startled as if woken from a dream.

'It's such a nice day outside,' her mother said. 'You should be out by the water.'

'No, I shouldn't.'

Her mother had just been to the farmer's market. She hauled overstuffed bags of fruits and vegetables onto the kitchen countertop, oblivious to Cassie's mood. 'Are you hungry?' she asked. 'I'll make some lunch.'

'Mom,' Cassie said, and the way she said it finally captured her mother's attention.

'What is it?' she asked, and joined Cassie on the couch. 'What happened?'

'Just a scare. But I'm pretty sure it was the hunters.'

Her mother's face paled. 'So they're not stopping with Constance.'

Cassie shook her head. 'I'm afraid not. I need you to tell me what you know about them.' Cassie could hear the pleading in her own voice.

Her mother was visibly uneasy. 'I don't know much,' she said. 'But there is one story from when I was much younger.'

Cassie drew in her breath as quietly as possible. 'Go on.'

'Back when I was with your dad.'

Cassie tried to remain perfectly still, to not make the slightest sound, nothing that could disturb the delicate balance of this moment – a story about her father.

'We were on a road trip,' her mother said, staring straight ahead. 'With some friends. And we had a run-in with a hunter family. One of our friends was marked with an ancient hunter symbol.'

Cassie thought back to the symbol she saw on Constance's forehead. 'The *W* inside the hexagon,' Cassie said.

'Yes.' Her mother swallowed hard. 'It's the way the hunters determine their victims. Once you've been marked, it's nearly impossible to escape ultimate death.'

Cassie made no reaction. She let her mother continue.

'But your father saved my friend. And we all escaped.'

'So he wasn't all bad,' Cassie said.

Her mother tried to smile. 'He was powerful. People were afraid of his intensity, but when he cared about something, he was fiercely loyal to it.'

Her voice quivered. 'And he was charming. I couldn't resist him, and I loved that I was all his and he was all mine. I was special in his eyes. That's how I got him to save my friend from the witch hunters. He did it all for me. He would have done anything for me.'

A single tear fled down her cheek like a winding river. She quickly wiped it away with the top of her finger. 'Ultimately, he put his desires in front of everyone else's, but there was a reason I was with him in the first place.'

This was a totally new side of Cassie's father, a side she had never known, never even considered. And she suddenly realised something. Her mother had genuinely loved John Blake. Real love. The way Cassie loved Adam. The kind of love that doesn't go away just because the person turns out to be different than you thought.

When Cassie reflected on this, she understood why it was so difficult for her mother to talk about him. It wasn't that she was being distant or secretive; she was still *hurting*.

Cassie threw her arms around her mother and squeezed her too hard. 'Thank you for telling me,' she said. 'About him.'

Cassie sat thinking, trying to process all she'd just learned. She tried to picture what her mother was like when she was happy and in love. And she imagined what it would be like now if her parents were still together. But in this mental picture her father was a regular man, a husband and a father – not a force of evil. It was wishful thinking, in no way useful to Cassie now. Whether or not he was ever good, Cassie had to remind herself of what her father had done.

'I wish I knew more about the hunters that would be helpful,' her mother said.

Her eyes glazed over for a moment and Cassie assumed their conversation was over. But then her mother said, 'We can leave, you know, if you want to. We don't have to stay in this town.'

'I can't leave,' Cassie said, taken aback. 'And you know that.'

'I thought that once, too,' her mother said. 'But it isn't true. You can always leave.'

Cassie moved carefully towards her mother. 'You're the one who brought me here, remember?'

'And I can be the one to take you away.' Her mother met her eyes sharply now.

'I won't run away,' Cassie said, her voice cracking with emotion.

'You won't run away because of Adam.' Her mother said it as a statement rather than a question. As if it were a weakness that she knew too well.

'I won't run away because I took an oath,' Cassie said.

Her mother started crying again, not just one single tear this time but many, as if a dam had broken inside her.

'I never wanted this for you,' she said. 'This is exactly what I've spent my entire life trying to protect you from.'

'I know.' Cassie strived to sound unafraid. 'But the best way you can protect me now is to keep talking to me, keep telling me things I need to know from the past, even if they're hard to talk about. Because I don't have anyone else to tell me these things but you.'

Her mother opened her arms and Cassie let herself be held.

'I promise you, Cassie,' her mother said. 'All I want is for you to be safe.'

They cried together for a little while, holding each other. It felt to Cassie like they were in mourning, grieving a death, and perhaps in a way they were. The death of the protective silence between them, and of their secrets and lies. The death of normalcy. Her mother rubbed soft circles into her back and told her everything would be okay, that they were in this together. For the first time, Cassie felt like a daughter.

Later that night, Cassie went to Adam's to tell him about the hunters' attack on the beach. They rarely hung out at his house and she was happy for the change of scenery. She loved being in his bedroom. Lying on his bed, she couldn't help but imagine him sleeping there, wrapped in those same sheets, with his features softening innocently as he dreamed. She gazed around the room and observed his things, everyday items that would have no meaning to her if they didn't belong to him – his schoolbooks stacked on his desk, his sneakers piled haphazardly in the closet and a pair of jeans strewn on the floor. She could almost see him coming home from school, tossing the books down, kicking off his shoes and stepping out of his jeans into something more comfortable. She felt an affection for the whole scene as she imagined it, and for every object he touched – by extension, it was all a part of him.

Adam returned to the room with some snacks and drinks in hand. He closed the door behind him.

'Sorry it's a little messy in here,' he said. 'I tried to clean it up, but . . .'

'It's perfect just like this,' Cassie said.

He joined her on the bed and she had the sudden urge to start rubbing his shoulders, to kiss his face and his neck – to forget all about the awful storm on the beach.

Adam's breathing slowed and Cassie could sense he was thinking the same thing. He swept his fingers suggestively across her thigh.

'You look beautiful tonight,' he said. 'But I've been worried about you. What happened today?' His hand slid from her thigh up to her hipbone, which was his favourite place to touch her.

Cassie took a deep breath and sat up. 'I went for a walk on the beach and I ran into Nick,' she said. Cassie paused to read Adam's expression, but his face remained neutral.

'And I was glad to see him,' she continued, 'because you know I've been trying to repair my friendship with him any way I can. But we'd just got to talking when the sky turned black and this awful storm started. We knew immediately by the looks of it that it was something supernatural.'

'The hunters,' Adam said.

Cassie nodded. 'We couldn't get away fast enough. Lightning bolts were flying straight for us. One would have . . .'

Cassie felt herself get choked up. She struggled to swallow down the knot that had formed in her throat. 'Nick risked his life to save me, Adam. I would have been hit if he hadn't acted so quickly to push me out of the way.'

Lines formed on Adam's forehead, but he stared straight down at the bedspread.

'He proved himself a real friend in that moment,'

Cassie said. 'To both of us. Don't you think?'

Adam continued looking down for a moment before raising his eyes to meet hers. 'Yes, you're right,' he said, and then shifted uncomfortably.

Cassie could see by the way he tightened his jaw that he was bothered it was Nick who had saved her, but he would never say that. 'I wish I'd been there, but I'm glad you're okay.' Adam took her hands and massaged them in his own. He brought them to his lips and kissed them. 'I don't know what I would have done if you'd been hurt.'

He kissed the inside of her wrist and up her forearm. Cassie knew where this was leading. As difficult as it was, she forced herself to remove her arm from his grasp.

'There's more,' she said. 'I talked to my mom. Really talked to her.'

Adam refocused his attention and sat up straight. 'And?'

'She told me about my father. You know he wasn't all bad, Adam. She really loved him.'

Adam seemed unsure of how to react. Black John was always a touchy subject between them.

'I know how that sounds,' Cassie said. 'But try to imagine it. Being in love with someone the way we are, truly in love, and then losing that person to the dark side.'

Adam shook his head. 'I don't want to imagine that.'

'Neither do I, so think about how awful it must have been for my poor mother.' Cassie could feel her emotions getting the best of her, and she fought the urge to start crying.

Adam reached for her hands again. 'I can hardly think of anything worse,' he said. 'But it's good that you can understand it now. I'm glad you had this breakthrough with your mom.'

Cassie let her eyes wander around Adam's room. For some reason it was difficult to look at him just then. Instead, she focused on the poster taped to his wall, of some band she'd never heard of.

'I'm sure your father was easy to fall in love with,' Adam said. 'He was a charismatic man, a natural leader. Your mother's smart – she wouldn't have been with him otherwise. It wasn't her fault, what happened.'

Sometimes Adam knew just what to say. It was a subtle shift in Cassie's mind, but all of a sudden she felt at ease. If Adam didn't blame her mother, in a way that meant he didn't blame Cassie either. She locked eyes with his and reached for him.

The Divide

'The important thing is that you're okay,' Adam said, allowing himself to be drawn in. 'And that we're together.'

Cassie lay back and Adam curled up next to her, pulling her close. She loved him so much, it almost ached. She felt she could never get enough of him.

Adam kissed her passionately and then paused for a moment. 'With everything going on,' he said. 'I'm just relieved—'

Cassie put her fingers over his mouth to quiet him. 'Enough talking,' she said, and pulled him closer.

Chapter Fourteen

'Okay,' Diana said. 'We don't have much time. Who has something to report?'

The Circle was eating lunch in their new spot, a small patch of woods up one of the narrow paths on the edge of the school grounds – a green grass hideaway beneath the cover of high birches and leafy apple blossoms. Adam suggested it as their new lunchtime turf for the warm-weather months.

All eyes turned to the Henderson brothers. They'd had a mission this morning: to set off a stink bomb in third-period maths. The plan was to be sent to the new principal's office together, where they could then tag team and look for evidence. The Circle was looking into anyone new in town, but the principal was number one on their list of potential hunters.

'Shouldn't we wait for Faye?' Deborah asked as she unpacked her lunch.

'Lately all we do is wait for Faye,' Melanie said. 'If she's got better places to be, then we should go on without her.'

'I can hear you,' Faye called out from the top of the path. She made her way down slowly.

'As I was saying.' Diana raised her voice. 'Chris, Doug, did you find anything?'

Faye made it down the path just in time to nudge Doug in the ribs with her pointy black boot. 'Go ahead, say it. You came up with nothing.'

'We came up with nothing,' Chris said while Doug remained silent. 'But not due to lack of trying. Mr Boylan seems like a pretty straight-up guy.'

'I don't buy it,' Nick said. 'He comes into town and everything blows up. It's too much of a coincidence. We should question him, push the investigation further.'

Cassie noticed Nick was looking at her when he said it.

'There's no need to be reckless,' Diana said.

Nick guffawed. 'Yeah there is.'

Nick was immeasurably different from Adam, who was so righteous, always. Even his adventure-seeking was based in devotion; never for a moment was it a form of revolt.

As Cassie watched Adam now, she observed how he scrambled around the group, always the mediator, trying to keep the peace above all else. The unity of the Circle meant more to him than anything.

That was it. That was the thing rolling around in the back of her mind since they'd argued the other night, the thing she couldn't quite put her finger on. But now that it occurred to her, it rang out with indisputable truth: Nothing came before the Circle to Adam. Not even her.

As if her discreet competition with Diana weren't enough, Cassie realised she would also be eternally pitted against the Circle as if it were another woman – a woman with greater hold over Adam's loyalty. How could she have not realised this sooner?

Diana, who'd barely touched her salad, glanced at Adam now and then cleared her throat. 'And has everyone been avoiding Outsiders, like we discussed?'

Cassie threw her peanut butter and jelly down onto her napkin. 'You don't have to be so vague, Diana. Everyone knows which Outsiders you mean.'

Melanie and Laurel looked down at their lunches. Cassie's sudden and uncharacteristic insolence obviously made them uncomfortable. Suzan and Sean glanced at each other with widened eyes, and Deborah's face tightened. But Nick, Cassie noticed, was grinning, amused by her outburst.

'Catfight,' Faye called out, rubbing her palms together. 'Now remember, ladies, no hair pulling.'

But Diana remained poised as always and revealed no defensiveness in her reply. 'That rule applies to all Outsiders equally, Cassie. It's not just about you being friends with Scarlett.'

Cassie felt her cheeks redden and her neck heat up. 'You have to believe me,' she said with a shaky voice. 'There's nothing sketchy about Scarlett. Just because she's an Outsider doesn't make her against us.'

'It doesn't?' Faye said sardonically.

'You can't say that for sure,' Diana insisted. 'We barely know anything about Scarlett.'

'Yes, I can.' Cassie was yelling now. 'I know what I see when I look at her. And I trust my sight.'

It was a low blow for Cassie to mention her sight – a reminder to Diana that it was Cassie alone who had the gift of psychic visions.

'Look out,' Faye said. 'Cassie's bringing out the big guns.'

'Your sight may be clouded,' Diana said rigidly.

But Cassie shot right back. 'Clouded by what?'

'By the fact that you've been obsessed with her since the second you met.' Diana snapped at last, losing her cool.

'Aha.' Faye clapped her hands together. 'Finally the truth comes out. Diana's jealous Cassie found a new best friend!'

A round of snickering passed through the group. Suzan and Deborah both nodded approvingly.

'A fault in the flawless marble that is our precious Diana,' Faye said. 'I love it.'

'I'm not jealous.' Diana settled her green eyes directly on Cassie.

'Yes, you are,' Cassie said.

Diana was rendered speechless by this final attack, but she refused to take her eyes away from Cassie's. Cassie wouldn't look away either. All the frustration and confusion and anger she'd felt over Diana's rejection of Scarlett and her going to Adam behind her back seemed to be flowing out of her now. And right back at her came Diana's disappointment and outrage over Cassie's audacity to defy her and the group. It was a standoff of wills. Was this what they had resorted to? This petty face-off? Nobody moved or said a word and, for a second, Cassie thought it could go on forever.

But then, of course, Adam got between them. 'Let's move on,' he said. 'We don't have much time and we still have lots to discuss. Diana, Deborah, tell us what happened when you followed Max.'

At the mention of Max's name, Faye lashed out, immediately furious. 'You did what?'

Diana had a new argument to deal with now, so she reharnessed all of her energy towards Faye. 'We haven't even accused Max of anything yet. No need to overreact.'

'I have every reason to overreact. You went behind my back.'

'He's an Outsider and he's new in town,' Deborah said. 'You knew he was on our list.'

'And we followed him straight to your house,' Diana said as calmly as still water.

Shock broke through the surface of the group, cracking them apart into a fissured hysteria. This meeting was turning out to be much more volatile than anyone anticipated.

'He was at your house?' Melanie's grey eyes flared.

'So that makes two people who've been breaking the

no-Outsider rule,' Laurel said with a tinge of antagonism in her usually peaceful voice.

Suzan blurted out with her mouth half full of Twinkie, 'But Max wanted nothing to do with Faye. He's been avoiding her for weeks.'

Deborah shook her head, disbelieving, 'Well, something changed. He's into her now. He dropped his whole *I'm too good for everyone* thing and was pawing after Faye like a needy puppy. He even ditched lacrosse practice to be with her. It was almost like he was under a spell . . .'

As soon as Deborah uttered the word *spell* it dawned on her and everyone.

Adam wielded his electric-blue eyes at Faye. 'You didn't,' he said. 'Tell me you didn't.'

But they all knew. That's what Faye had been up to all this time, making her late to meetings and secretive about plans. Faye did a love spell to get her crush.

'You swore,' Adam said. 'We all swore not to practise any magic.'

Faye waved Adam off with her long red nails as if to wipe him away from her sight. 'It was nothing. A simple love spell is hardly magic at all.'

Melanie went to Adam's side. She was angrier than

Cassie had ever seen her. 'They'll find us now, you know. The hunters.'

'Relax.' Faye laughed. 'They're not Cupid hunters. No one noticed. And no one will.'

'But any slip could mean we're outed,' Nick said. His hands were balled into fists and his breathing was heavy. 'We can't afford to make mistakes.'

Faye whipped around and rushed at Nick. 'Why don't you tell that to Cassie?'

'Cassie hasn't done anything wrong. You have.' Nick squeezed his fists tighter.

'Are you sure?' Faye shoved Nick forcefully in the chest.

'That's enough,' Diana screamed out. 'This discussion is getting us nowhere and we all have to get back to class. We'll pick this up later.'

But how? Cassie thought. How could they possibly pick up all these broken pieces? Everyone gathered their trash slowly and began making their way back to the school building, but Faye stayed put. 'Seriously? You're all leaving? The fun was just getting started.'

Melanie elbow checked her on her way back to the path, but Faye remained unfazed. She called out to Cassie, amused, 'I like the new angry version of Melanie so much better than the boring old reasonable one, don't you?'

Cassie ignored her, stuffing the remaining bread from her sandwich back into its paper bag.

'The new jealous version of Diana isn't bad, either,' Faye continued. 'And the lying version of Cassie, well, that's not so new.'

It was what Faye wanted, to draw her into a fight, but Cassie couldn't ignore her any longer. She met Faye eye to eye. 'I don't know what you're talking about,' she said. 'And I don't care, either.'

Faye reached out and caught Cassie's chin with her strong fingers. 'You *should* care.'

Cassie resisted the urge to pull away. The red stone Faye wore around her throat reflected the sunlight into Cassie's eyes, burning them, but she held her gaze. 'I'm not afraid of you,' she said through Faye's grip.

'One more of your many stupid mistakes.' Faye squeezed her fingers tighter around Cassie's chin.

'Hey! Let her go.' It was Nick at the top of the path.

Laughing, Faye released her. 'This one can take care of herself, Nicholas. She doesn't need you saving her. Isn't that right, Cassie?'

Cassie climbed up the path to Nick's side as Faye

shouted, 'You'll never be Adam, Nicholas. No matter how hard you try.'

Cassie looked down the path at Faye, feeling the fire in her gut rise to her throat. 'Faye, you're pathetic. And deep inside, you're weak, far weaker than me. Don't push me to prove it.'

Faye licked her blood-red lips and then slid her tongue seductively across her teeth. 'That's more like it,' she said. 'Give me more of that dark side, Cassandra. That's what I want to see.'

Chapter Fifteen

It was a good ten-minute walk to the lighthouse, plenty of time for Cassie to work up her heart rate and fill her lungs with cold, fresh air. Some of the tension among the group from earlier had dissipated. Cassie thought Faye was being let off a little too easily after performing the love spell, but she was too relieved to see everyone getting along again to mention it. Besides, Cassie had also been forgiven for hanging out with Scarlett.

It was Diana who suggested the twelve of them walk to the lighthouse together in one large group, but they all wanted to do it. Driving was cool, Cassie thought, but there was nothing like sauntering up the street on a moonlit night in a huge pack of your closest friends. It made her feel invincible and part of something so much bigger and more important than herself.

The Divide

It was a full moon, and Laurel brought along a bag of fresh-baked cookies. It was an old family recipe of Laurel's that required the crushed leaves of an herb called mugwort, which had to be picked and ingested during a full moon. Laurel claimed the cookies improved divination, clairvoyance and psychic powers, but Cassie and the others stuffed their mouths full of them as they walked because they were delicious. All those other things were just bonuses.

Adam felt for Cassie's hand and, when he found it, she didn't pull away. Cassie had been on edge lately for sure, but for the moment everything felt fine and her connection to Adam was strong. His fingers wrapped around hers reassured her that in spite of all they had to fear, she wasn't in this alone, and together they could overcome anything.

The night was invigorating. The trees overhead smelled of sweet flowers and the ground beneath Cassie's shoes was moist with dew. A rare carelessness came over them as they walked. Not just Cassie and Adam but the whole group. They hollered up the street, goofing on one another and banging on garbage cans. Chris challenged Doug to race him the rest of the way and they all started running in order to judge the winner. They stopped short when they saw it and collectively gasped.

It seemed impossible. The lighthouse had been burned to the ground. In its place was a pile of soot and ash.

Irrationally, Cassie thought they must've arrived at the wrong location. How could a structure so sturdy and steadfast, so permanent in its vigilance, have melted down to this? But the anger in Adam's eyes forced Cassie to accept the harder truth. Not only was the lighthouse gone, but someone had destroyed it on purpose.

Melanie spoke first. 'That was a historical landmark,' she said. 'It's been there for, like, three hundred years.'

'That's what you're thinking about right now?' Nick said. 'How about how the hunters knew exactly where to find us?'

Diana placed her hand gently on Nick's shoulder. 'Hold on, we shouldn't jump to conclusions. We don't know for sure it was the hunters.'

Nick shrugged off Diana's hand. 'This was a message, loud and clear. How much clearer would you like them to be?'

Diana turned to Melanie and Laurel. 'You two were the last ones here, weren't you? Are you sure you didn't accidentally leave any candles burning?'

Melanie's eyes widened. 'Are you accusing *us* of

burning down the lighthouse?'

'I'm not accusing,' Diana said. 'Just asking.'

Cassie couldn't stand to listen to any more arguing. She made her way over the grass, towards the edge of where the entrance to the cottage once stood.

Cassie heard Adam come to Diana's defence against Melanie and Laurel. 'It would be better for all of us if you had been the ones to burn it down,' he said. 'Then at least we'd know for sure it was an accident and not an act of—'

'It wasn't an accident,' Cassie called out to them. Her voice echoed over the space between them like an ocean wave. Right where the entrance to the light keeper's cottage once stood was a symbol burned in ash on the ground. It was the same symbol that appeared on Constance's forehead.

Adam was the first to reach her. 'The hunter symbol,' he said, just in time for the others to fall in line behind him. They saw it now, too. They couldn't not see it.

'The coven has been marked,' Cassie said.

'Faye, this is all your fault,' Nick shouted out. 'Because you had to do magic.'

For once Adam agreed with Nick. 'They tracked your love spell.'

'I told you,' Melanie said. 'I told you this would happen.'

'That's enough!' Faye's eyes flamed with rage. 'What makes you all so sure it was my fault?'

She pointed her longest red fingernail at Diana. 'You're always so careful not to jump to conclusions. Stop for a moment, call off the dogs and think of who could have actually done this.'

Then Faye twisted her neck around to glare at Cassie while keeping her shoulders squared to Diana. 'I think Scarlett would be a reasonable suspect,' she said. 'Especially since Cassie brought her here just the other day.'

Cassie remained silent.

'I saw you,' Faye said.

'Don't try to turn this on me,' Cassie said, but that was all she could say. She couldn't deny it.

Adam and Diana stared at Cassie with identical expressions of disbelief.

'Is that true?' Adam asked. 'You brought Scarlett to the lighthouse?

Cassie looked down at the horrible symbol burned into the ground, with its serpentine *W* and satanic-looking hexagon. This wasn't the work of Scarlett. She was sure of that.

'Cassie, how could you?' Diana couldn't contain her exasperation.

Cassie looked pleadingly into Diana's infuriated eyes. 'She was with me when I dropped off some herbs for Melanie and Laurel,' Cassie said. 'But I didn't let her inside and I didn't tell her anything. I swear to you, she had nothing to do with this.'

'You weren't supposed to be seeing Scarlett at all,' Melanie said. 'And you brought her to our sacred space.'

Faye was thoroughly enjoying the bloodbath she started. How easy it had been to divert the attention away from her forbidden love spell. Faye addressed the group. 'What Cassie has done is unforgivable,' she said malevolently. 'She betrayed us.'

'You betrayed us, too, Faye,' Cassie said. 'And how would you even know I brought Scarlett to the lighthouse unless you were spying on me?'

'That's not really the point,' Diana interjected. 'I agree with Faye on this. Bringing Scarlett to the lighthouse was a betrayal. And we need to unify now more than ever. No Outsiders can be trusted, no matter what.'

Cassie lost the little bit of control she'd had left. 'So let me get this straight,' she said. 'Your idea of unification is siding with Faye?'

Adam replied on Diana's behalf. 'It's for your own safety, Cassie. Scarlett isn't one of us. And under no circumstances did she belong anywhere near our meeting place.'

'Maybe it's me who isn't one of you,' Cassie blurted out before she could stop herself.

That was the last straw for Diana. She screamed then like Cassie had never imagined she could. 'Of course you're one of us, Cassie. You're more crucial to this Circle than any of us. Don't you think we all realise that?'

Then Diana turned to Faye. 'And you're not off the hook either. Cassie's right that you also betrayed the group. Max is off limits and so is your magic.'

'Or else what?' Faye said.

Diana didn't even blink. 'Or else you forfeit your privileges as a leader of this Circle.'

A few seconds passed before Adam broke the deathly silence. 'The coven has been marked,' he said. 'But do the hunters know who we are, individually?'

'Good question,' Melanie said. 'But either way, we have to figure out a way to fight them.'

'That's right,' Diana said. Her voice regained its angelic timbre. 'And I wanted to share something very important with you all tonight. Before all these surprises.'

She looked at Cassie and then at Faye, scolding them each individually with her eyes. Then she dug through her bag and pulled out her Book of Shadows.

'I found a spell,' she said. 'A spell to destroy witch hunters.'

'What?' Adam asked, sounding outraged Diana had kept this discovery from him. 'Why didn't you say anything sooner?'

'I wasn't sure if it was what I thought it was,' Diana said in her defence. 'The text was mostly in Latin and needed to be translated. But now I'm sure. That's why I wanted to meet tonight, to tell you all at once.'

'Let's perform the spell right now,' Melanie said, sounding hopeful for the first time in days.

Diana shook her head. 'First we have to know for sure who the hunters are.'

Nick shot Chris and Doug a look. 'Let's do it on the principal. We're sure enough.'

'No.' Diana's green eyes flared. 'The spell will only work on a real hunter. If we try it on someone who isn't one of them, we'll only be exposing ourselves as witches. Not to mention hurting someone innocent.'

'Wow, that's big news,' Faye said. 'We have a spell we can't use.'

'We will use it.' Adam gave one last look at the symbol burned on the ground. 'When they strike again. At this point, I think we can count on that happening.'

'But what happens then?' Melanie asked. 'If we do this spell. Will the hunters die?'

Diana hesitated. 'It's a little unclear. The translation left a lot to interpretation, but it seems like the effect of the spell depends on the hunter.'

'So they might die,' Melanie said.

'Let me have a look at this.' Faye grabbed Diana's Book of Shadows from her hands and scanned the page. As her eyes moved back and forth across the ancient script, she appeared to be drawing in her breath and backing away from the words in disbelief.

'This isn't a spell,' Faye said. 'It's a curse.'

Diana stared at the ground. 'Yes,' she said. 'Technically it is a curse.'

Faye was suddenly roiling with excitement. 'It's similar to a deflection spell by turning the hunters' power back on them, but it calls on Hecate. This could be . . .' She couldn't find the right word.

'Dangerous,' Diana said. 'We'll only use it as a last resort.'

Chapter Sixteen

The rain was only a drizzle, and although it was night-time, people were out and about. Scarlett had invited Cassie out tonight. Of course Cassie declined, but she wished she didn't have to. That's just what Cassie needed to clear her head – she needed to see other people, non-witches. She decided to drive into town. Even if she couldn't join the crowds of people going about their normal lives, she could at least watch them from inside her Volkswagen.

But she'd barely made it to Bridge Street when the light rain amplified to a hammering downpour. Everyone out on the streets scrambled for shelter inside restaurants and stores; some hovered within doorways and beneath overpasses. Cassie was dry and safe inside her car, and she felt like she was inside a snow globe that someone had shaken up, submerged by the shuddering rain on all sides but also untouched by it.

And then she suddenly felt stripped of that safety. Her heart started to pound in her chest and she began to sweat. She felt like she was being followed, but she didn't see any cars behind her. She kept checking the rear-view mirror, but all she saw was the wet darkness in her own back window. Still, she decided to take a detour, in hopes of shaking the feeling.

With a sharp turn of the steering wheel, she veered onto Dodge Street, a secluded road that would lead her back to the turnpike. Cassie had to slow down to manoeuvre its many meandering curves, but when she stepped on the brake pedal, her foot emptily dropped to the floor.

She tried again and again, but there was no use. Her brakes weren't working.

The car suddenly felt to her like it was speeding up, an angry vessel set on racing her to her death. She couldn't stop it, and letting up on the gas pedal was only doing so much. Panicked, she gripped the steering wheel and tried to bear off to the side of the road, where maybe the grass would slow the car enough so she could jump out to safety.

But the grass did nothing to reduce the acceleration. Cassie's only chance was to jump out while the car continued full speed ahead. Panicked, she clutched the door handle and pushed the door open. But before she had the chance to leap to the ground, the car smashed right into a giant, thick-barked oak tree.

She blacked out for a moment, maybe longer. When she opened her eyes, she saw she'd been thrown from the car, through the windshield. She checked her arms and legs to see if she could move them and searched her face for blood. Unbelievably, she was all right.

But her car was totalled. Looking at it through the dark rain, it reminded Cassie of a crushed soda can, flimsily accordioned to the tree. It was a miracle to be alive.

She stood up slowly, continuing to take inventory of her surroundings, and recognised that the evil feeling was gone. Whatever dark presence had been following her had disappeared, but Cassie couldn't shake the feeling that this was no accident.

She welled up with tears then. It wasn't a miracle. It was the protection spell that had saved her.

Cassie hated to do it, but she knew she had to. She checked her body and clothes for that awful ancient symbol. It reminded her of searching for deer ticks after a day out in the woods, except the consequences in this case meant ultimate death. She was relieved not to find one. Cassie may have nearly been killed tonight, but at least she hadn't been marked.

With shaking hands, Cassie pulled out her cell phone to call for help. But out in the middle of nowhere, she couldn't get a signal. Cassie started to panic even more. She was stranded out here, a sitting target.

Cassie never should have gone out alone, without telling anyone where she was going. She was naive to think the hunters wouldn't come after her again the first chance they had. There was no escaping them.

Cassie couldn't stop shaking while she waited in the pouring rain, hoping a kind stranger would drive by. But every sound and shadow made her jump at the alternative, and she grew stiff as a silver car slowed to a stop before her. But then Cassie recognised the face inside. It was Scarlett.

'Oh my goodness, are you all right?' Scarlett jumped out of her car and ran to Cassie, leaving the door open. 'Are you hurt?'

'I'm okay,' Cassie said, breathing a sigh of relief at a familiar face.

Scarlett hugged her close to her chest, nearly as stupefied by the sight of the crushed car as Cassie was. 'You could have been killed,' she said. 'And you're soaking wet!'

She dashed to the trunk of her car and retrieved an enormous wool blanket. She wrapped it around Cassie and rubbed her arms until they warmed.

Cassie was too freaked out by the accident to resist.

'You're okay,' Scarlett said in a voice as comforting as the thick wool around Cassie's shoulders. 'I'll take you home.'

The next day at school, everyone was talking about Cassie's recent brush with death. It was like the accident brought her popularity points in a sick and twisted way. Even Portia Bainbridge made her way through the crowded hallway to catch a look at Cassie at her locker. She turned her thin nose up at Cassie and narrowed her cold hazel eyes. 'So glad you didn't mess up that pretty little face of yours when you flew through the windshield,' she said.

The thought crossed Cassie's mind: could Portia have cut the brakes in her car, or was it one of her moose-head brothers?

But Portia had retreated from messing with the Circle after their final blowout last autumn. Since then she'd been distracted by a new boyfriend and barely seemed to think about much else. And her brothers, Jordan and Logan, were both at college. Cassie would have heard if they'd been back around the island.

Just then, Sally Waltman stepped to Cassie's side. A head shorter than Portia, Sally still crossed her wiry arms with the fierceness of a taller, stronger person. 'She's been through enough, Portia,' Sally said. 'She doesn't need your harassment on top of it.'

Portia scowled. 'Don't forget which side you're on, Sally. You don't want to start being confused for one of them, or you might get hurt.'

'Let it go already.' Sally forcefully took Portia by the arm and urged her away. 'Come on, we're going to be late,' she said, and shot Cassie a look of apology over her shoulder.

Sally standing up to Portia meant a lot, considering she'd once been one of the Circle's most hated enemies. If the group's relationship with Sally could come this far, she didn't see why they couldn't be more accepting of other well-meaning Outsiders, like Scarlett. Not all of them were as vile as Portia. Why couldn't the Circle see that?

* * *

At lunch, the group gathered at their spot in the woods and grilled Cassie for details. She told them about the bad feeling that came over her just before the accident and how her brakes failed, but some details she kept to herself. She was exhausted, both physically and emotionally, and she couldn't handle what their reaction would be if she told them about Scarlett showing up just after the crash.

'But were there any clues about who the hunters were that did this?' Diana asked.

'No,' Cassie said. 'None.'

'I saw Portia harassing you at your locker this morning,' Nick called out. 'She's been off our radar too long. I don't trust it.'

Diana looked doubtful but said, 'It couldn't hurt to consider Portia and her brothers possible suspects.'

'And Sally Waltman,' Suzan said.

Diana shook her head. 'Sally's been pretty straightforward with us. Of all the Outsiders, I think she'd be the least likely to want to hurt us.'

'You guys are getting sidetracked,' Deborah said. 'These hunters are strong. Whoever they are, they weren't in town before now, or we would have known it.'

Melanie agreed. 'That ancient symbol didn't come from any of our old schoolmates.'

Adam had been pacing back and forth the way he always did when he was nervous. He hadn't calmed down since he learned of the accident. 'I still wish you could have called me,' he said to Cassie. 'How'd you even get home?'

Cassie hesitated.

It was a simple question. There was no need for such a long pause and the entire group picked up on it.

Adam stiffened and turned accusingly to Nick. 'Did she call you? Were you the one to drive her home?'

Nick appeared blindsided by Adam's accusation, but he quickly mirrored Adam's aggressive posture with his own. 'No, she didn't. But I wish she had,' he said.

'Stop it, both of you.' Cassie didn't have a choice. She had to tell them the truth.

'I didn't call anyone to come pick me up.' She paused, not wanting to go on. Cassie looked down at her shoes. *Run*, she thought. Just run away from this awful moment. But there was nowhere to run to, and she knew it. Almost inaudibly she said, 'Scarlett happened to drive by while I was stranded. She drove me home.'

Adam shook his head, sidestepping Nick, who'd also

dropped his bravado. Diana reached for a nearby tree to steady herself. They were speechless, but Faye had the words right at hand to announce what the whole group was thinking.

'Oh, yeah,' she said. 'Scarlett just happened to drive by, finding you in the middle of nowhere. What a lucky coincidence!'

Cassie wasn't having it. The last person she owed an explanation to was Faye. She stepped to her boldly. 'Why would she have helped me if she'd been the one trying to hurt me?'

'You're being stupid,' Deborah said, not holding back an ounce of disgust. 'It can't be a coincidence.'

'She's not being stupid,' Diana said. 'Cassie's just blinded. She wants to see the best in Scarlett.'

'Exactly. Which is just plain stupid,' Deborah insisted.

'No,' Cassie said. 'Scarlett is innocent, I swear.'

Diana frowned at her sympathetically. 'I'm sorry, Cassie. But it's too suspicious that Scarlett would just happen to know where you were last night after the accident. This appears to be the proof we've been looking for all along.'

'It's the principal,' Cassie shouted. 'I can feel it in my bones.'

The Secret Circle

Adam responded to Cassie softly, guardedly. 'We haven't been able to dig up a single suspicious thing on the new principal. He's clean, Cassie.'

Even Adam wasn't willing to side with Cassie this time. She could plead with him, with all of them, all afternoon, but it was useless – they'd already made up their minds to not believe her. Cassie turned to Nick desperately, thinking if anyone might back her up, it would be him. But Nick was stone-faced, unwilling to rebel against the status quo on this.

Faye rose up and positioned herself in the middle of their huddle. 'I say we go down to the docks after school and have a word with Scarlett.'

'We should do the witch-hunter curse on her,' Deborah yelled out.

Diana went to Faye's side, crossed her arms over her chest and nodded. 'I agree,' she said. 'Who's with us?'

An assemblage of hands went up.

'But we should have a full Circle to do it. Otherwise we might not be strong enough.' Diana beheld Cassie in her gaze. 'So are we a complete Circle or not?'

Cassie turned to Adam. His eyes were filled with longing and love, urging her to trust them, to trust him. And she wanted to trust Adam, she really did.

'Cassie,' Nick said, 'if Scarlett's not a hunter, the spell won't work on her. This could be your chance to prove yourself right.' He smiled gently, giving a nod towards Diana and Adam. 'And prove them wrong.'

'That's true,' Melanie said to Diana. 'If we perform the curse on Scarlett and she's not a hunter, then she'll know what we are.'

'I know that,' Diana said with confidence.

Cassie raised her eyes to Diana's. 'You're that sure,' she said, 'that you'd be willing to expose the Circle to a harmless, good-intentioned Outsider.'

'I'm that sure.' Diana stared back at Cassie without anger or hatred, but with utter conviction.

'Then I'm with you,' Cassie said in a hushed tone, almost to herself. 'We'll go to the docks after school today.'

Chapter Seventeen

The group cruised along the picturesque coastline of the New Salem waterfront until they reached the docks where Scarlett worked. On the way, Diana had taken Cassie aside and thanked her for coming with them. She said she felt bad about going against Cassie's wishes, but insisted it was for the safety of the group as a whole.

Cassie forced herself to sound agreeable and said she understood. What use was it bumping heads with Diana now? And besides, like Nick said, this encounter might prove once and for all that Scarlett was just a regular girl with no intentions of harming the Circle. Then Cassie would be free to be her friend.

Overhearing Cassie and Diana's apparent truce, Adam took Cassie's hand in his. He was still holding it now as Diana addressed the group.

'Are we all clear on the plan?' Diana asked. Her blonde hair shimmered in the sun and she had the self-possession of a commander-in-chief.

Deborah's eyes gleamed with the desire for combat. 'We draw her out, we circle her and then we cast the witch-hunter curse.'

'No,' Adam corrected Deborah. 'We circle her, and we get all the facts.'

'That's right,' Diana said. 'We should try to get as much information out of her before we cast the curse.' She paused. 'Especially since we're not entirely sure what'll happen once we do.'

Cassie couldn't think about that part. The only way she would get through this was by continuing to believe in Scarlett.

'There she is.' Laurel pointed to the side exit of the Oyster Bar. 'She must be on a break.'

'Perfect,' Faye said. It was plain to see that her blood was boiling with excitement. She charged ahead of the group, leading the way.

Scarlett saw them coming almost immediately. Anyone in their right mind would have become alarmed at the sight of this angry mob of twelve approaching, but Scarlett smiled wide and started waving to them, heaving her skinny arm back and forth as if she needed to catch their attention.

'She's bluffing,' Faye said as they continued their approach. 'Don't fall for it.'

But Faye didn't even have to say it. Not one of them faltered or fell out of step. Before Scarlett could even say 'Hello,' they had her surrounded.

Finally she began to catch on that something peculiar was happening, that she was in trouble. 'What's going on?' she asked, turning, circling, trying to locate Cassie in the ring of heavy-breathing bodies around her.

The scene couldn't have gone down more smoothly. They were positioned on the side of the Oyster Bar, where it was desolate except for the occasional busboy going to the dumpsters. Scarlett was trapped. No one would even hear her scream.

Only Cassie could save her now.

'Scarlett,' she said. 'We need the truth from you, or else you're going to get hurt. My friends think you had something to do with my car accident. I don't believe that. But I need you to prove to them that you're innocent.'

Scarlett's round, dark eyes softened. 'Is that what this is about? Of course I had nothing to do with that.'

'What about the lighthouse?' Diana's voice was stern.

It sounded more like a threat than a question.

'What about it?' Scarlett asked.

'You burned it to the ground,' Faye shouted.

'I what?' Scarlett began to lose her cool. 'Why would I do something like that?' Her survival instincts set in and Cassie knew that it wasn't far off now, the moment of truth.

Adam narrowed in on her. 'Who are you working with?'

'At the Oyster Bar?' Scarlett was trembling now, like a cornered street cat poised to strike.

'Answer the question,' Diana said. 'Who are you working with?'

'I don't know what you're talking about!' Scarlett cried out and ran for Cassie then, for help. The Circle moved in closer on her, blocking any exit. But Faye saw Scarlett's rushing at Cassie as a direct threat and swiftly reacted. She raised her hands and called out, 'By the power of this Circle, I call on Hecate!'

Time slowed down for Cassie in that moment. She could see the shock on Scarlett's face and the fury in Faye's eyes. She could hear Diana screaming out, *'No, not yet!'*

But Faye was unstoppable. She appeared to take on giant proportions the instant she called on Hecate, as if she embodied the form of the dark Goddess herself. She seemed to grow to seven feet tall, and her honey-coloured eyes blackened like marbles. She cast the first part of the witch-hunter curse with the power of thunder.

Curse this ancient hunter who aims to harm me
Acts of evil now return threefold to thee!

The sky above Faye's outstretched hands reddened and spiralled into a violent funnel-like cloud. She harnessed it towards her, drew it in and moulded it with one swirl of her charmed fingertips into a ball of fire. As she tossed it from one hand to the other, the Circle chanted the Latin words they'd memorised – dark, unfathomable words they barely understood – until Faye heaved the fireball at Scarlett like a heavy stone.

But Scarlett shocked them all. With one swift motion she caught the roiling fire in her hands and burst it between her palms. 'Be it undone!' she called out, the classic defence spell.

Within seconds, Faye shrunk back down to size and toppled over sideways onto the ground. The opening in the sky stitched itself closed and the light of day returned to normal.

'How do you know the defence spell?' Cassie asked.

But even as the question left Cassie's lips, she knew there could only be one explanation. Scarlett wasn't a witch hunter. She was a witch, like them.

Deborah and Suzan ran to Faye to see if she was okay. Slowly, they got Faye to her feet, but she appeared dazed and wobbly.

Scarlett turned to Cassie. Her dark eyes were still inflamed from the spell. 'I'm sorry you had to find out this way,' she said.

Adam stepped forward, astonished. 'You're a witch?'

Scarlett nodded and turned again to Cassie. 'I wanted to tell you since the moment we first met.'

'Why didn't you?' Diana asked.

'I was waiting for the right time,' Scarlett said.

'You're a witch?' Cassie asked, repeating Adam's words and stunned tone verbatim.

'Not just any witch.' Scarlett smiled shyly. 'I'm your half-sister.'

'What?' Cassie could hardly breathe. 'How?'

'We have the same father,' she said. 'Black John.'

Scarlett observed the shock in each of their faces. 'I came to this town trying to escape the witch hunters, just like you are now. Back home, we were discovered.'

She turned to Diana, somehow understanding she was the Circle's leader. 'The hunters killed my mother,' she said. 'And they marked me. I came here to get the protection of the Circle.'

'So you knew about us,' Melanie said.

'Yes.' Scarlett reached for Cassie and took both her hands in her own. 'My mother grew up in this town. I've known I had a sister out here my entire life and I wanted to meet her.'

This was almost more than Cassie could bear. The whole world started to spin and she thought she might actually be dreaming, but then Diana spoke up, loudly jolting her from her haze. 'So Cassie was right all along,' she said.

Diana put one slender hand on Cassie's shoulder and the other on Scarlett's. 'Please accept my apology,' she said. 'Our apology. To both of you. We should have had more faith.'

'I accept,' Scarlett said, smiling.

But Faye's husky voice crashed the sentimental moment. Apparently, she'd regained her strength. 'How do we know you're not lying, Scarlett? What proof do you have for any of these claims?'

Deborah answered for Scarlett and for the group.

'When she knocked you on your behind by deflecting your curse,' she said, 'that was proof enough for me.'

'Me too,' Suzan said, laughing.

Faye smirked. 'I mean about being Cassie's half-sister.'

'She's telling the truth,' Cassie said. 'I think, deep down, I've known it all along.'

Diana turned to Faye. 'I think it's time for us to trust Cassie on this. Obviously, her sight wasn't clouded after all.'

One by one, everyone expressed their apologies to Scarlett. Even Melanie, who'd wanted so badly to believe Scarlett had been the hunter responsible for killing her great-aunt Constance, put aside her desire for retribution and shook her hand.

'We misjudged you,' Melanie said. 'I'm sorry.'

It was hardly enough, considering they'd just tried to kill her, but it was all anyone could say.

The apologies were for Cassie, too. But Cassie didn't need anyone's apology – she had been right. She knew she felt connected to Scarlett, she just knew it! What a relief it was to have the truth come out at last.

Adam appeared as relieved as she was. He went to Cassie and wrapped his arms around her.

'I should have never doubted you,' he said.

'That's okay,' Cassie said. 'You can remember that for next time.' She hugged Adam back and, as she did, she caught sight of Nick looking on. He was the only one who'd stuck with her when everyone else was so sure Scarlett was evil. She would have to remember to thank him later, when they had a moment alone together.

Chapter Eighteen

Cassie had always dreamed of having a sister, of having someone *to* confide in and share secrets with, someone who would always stick by her no matter what. Cassie and Diana had promised to be sisters to each other, the sisters neither of them had. But that wasn't going so well these days, or at least not like they thought it would. But now she had this, a real sister. Well, a half-sister, but still, Scarlett was *real*. Cassie wasn't an only child any more.

That night, Cassie invited Scarlett to sleep over at her house. She had this urge to learn everything she could about her as soon as possible. Not to grill Scarlett on what she knew of their father and the witch hunters, though of course that was important, too, but everything about *her*. There was plenty of time for Scarlett to share everything she knew about the hunters with the Circle. But tonight was just about them. They deserved that much.

Cassie's mother was away visiting friends in Cape Cod, so the girls had the whole house to themselves. Cassie was relieved, because she wasn't sure yet how to broach the subject of Scarlett with her mother. How exactly does one even begin such a conversation? 'Mom, the love of your life, who turned out to be evil? He also had another child.' Especially with a mother like Cassie's, who would always rather hide from the past and pretend it doesn't exist. Her mother would stick her head in the sand like an ostrich and live that way forever if she could. Finding out Cassie had a half-sister and worse, that her husband had another daughter with a different woman, might be more than she could handle. It would take a lot of groundwork on Cassie's behalf to prepare her mother for such a shock.

But for tonight, they could just be sisters. She felt herself slip into an immediate playfulness, as if she and Scarlett were trying to make up for the childhood they had been robbed of sharing. For the first few hours, they did all the traditional sleepover things. They ordered a pepperoni pizza and laughed too loud. They painted each other's nails with sparkly purple nail polish and wolfed down chocolate ice-cream sundaes till they had stomach aches.

Then they both changed into their pyjamas and Scarlett pinned Cassie's hair back in two intertwined French braids. Cassie brushed through Scarlett's long waves of wild red hair and couldn't help but ask, 'If you didn't dye your hair, would it be the same colour as mine?'

'Yup,' Scarlett said. 'Look at our eyebrows; they're the same shade of brown.'

'And our noses are shaped the same.'

'That's true,' Scarlett said. 'We both have the same perfect button noses.'

'Do you hate peas?' Cassie asked ridiculously.

'I do, but I don't think that's genetic.'

'You don't understand.' Cassie was giggling uncontrollably. 'I hate peas so much, I swear it's in my DNA.'

Scarlett cracked up.

Having a sleepover with Scarlett was nothing at all like having one with Diana. Diana always behaved like a serious adult. She rarely loosened up enough to just be silly. But silliness was no problem for Scarlett. Even though she was a witch, she didn't always act like one. And even though she'd suffered through intolerable tragedy and loss, she wasn't mired in sombreness. First and foremost, Scarlett was a girl who wanted to have a little fun, and that was a much-needed breath of fresh air to Cassie.

They stayed up late into the night talking. The outside world grew quiet and sleepy and finally silent while Cassie and Scarlett remained awake sharing stories. And as the hours passed, their conversation drifted into deeper waters. In hushed tones, Scarlett filled Cassie in on many of the gaps in their family history.

'I always sensed I was different,' she said. 'Even before I knew I was a witch.'

'I know what you mean, believe me.' Cassie brought her knees in towards her chest. 'I never felt at home anywhere. I always felt like a freak.'

'And the dreams and nightmares,' Scarlett said.

Cassie nodded. 'Mostly the nightmares.'

'And the strange things that would happen every time I got angry.' Scarlett's voice rose a bit. 'That was really the kicker.'

Cassie nodded more rapidly. The similarities between them were uncanny. Cassie wanted to tell Scarlett about the darkness she sometimes felt inside. Not only the bad feelings triggered by certain people, like the new principal, for example, but that other darkness. The one deep down that she could hardly admit to herself existed. Did Scarlett feel that, too? Did she fear there was some sinister piece of Black John lodged in her soul, infecting and clouding it like a cancerous smoker's lung? But before Cassie could muster up the courage to ask such a question, Scarlett's round face turned deathly serious.

'And when I first touched hematite,' she said. 'The feeling in my chest was—'

'I know!' Cassie screamed out. 'Me, too!'

'It's my working stone,' Scarlett said.

'Mine, too,' Cassie said.

Scarlett grinned knowingly, as if she suspected as much. 'It's a truly rare occurrence, you know. To have hematite as your working stone.'

Cassie turned away for a second, feeling ashamed. She had to remind herself that she didn't have to be embarrassed of her connection to Black John, at least not with Scarlett.

Scarlett watched her patiently. 'It's okay,' she said. 'I know this is a lot to digest.'

She does feel it, Cassie thought. Scarlett understood the mortification of Cassie's deepest secret. Scarlett endured that same crushing darkness dormant inside herself.

The air between them momentarily quieted and Cassie knew this was her chance to ask about their father. 'It's because of him,' she said. 'That hematite works for both of us. Right?'

Scarlett nodded. 'I'd say that's most likely the reason.'

'Did you know him?' Cassie asked, not having to utter their father's name.

Scarlett shook her head. 'No. But my mom told me stories. Didn't yours?'

Cassie blushed, shamed by her own mother's shortcomings. 'Not really.'

'Our moms were best friends growing up,' Scarlett said. 'Did you know that?'

Cassie searched her memory for any recollection of her mother talking about old friends, but she came up blank. 'No,' she said, disappointed. 'I don't know much at all about my mother's past.'

'Well, our moms were best friends,' Scarlett said matter-of-factly. 'Until Black John came between them. Your mom stole him from my mom. That's why my mom left town.'

'I had no idea.' Cassie's heart fell a little because of this new picture of her mother, but also because she suddenly thought of Diana and Nick, and how she and Adam came between them. Would things ever be the same between them, or were they bound for the same fate?

Scarlett noticed a change in Cassie's disposition. 'Have I upset you?' she asked. 'Maybe I'm saying too much too soon.'

'No, don't be silly.' Cassie forced herself to relax and to put Adam and the others out of her mind for now. 'I want to know everything. Don't hold anything back, please.'

Scarlett puckered her lips and eyed Cassie sceptically. 'We have our whole lives to catch up with each other, you know. We don't have to do it all in one night.'

It was an amazingly comforting thought. *Our whole lives*. They could go back to giggling and goofing around, and pick up this seriousness tomorrow. But Cassie had waited for this chance for far too long to let it go any longer. She needed to know the truth, about everything. 'Please tell me more,' she said. 'I can handle it.'

'Okay then.' Scarlett took Cassie's hand and squeezed it and, when she did, Cassie looked down at their intertwined fingers. It seemed like she could almost see a cord wrapping around their hands, connecting them. *Just like the connection between Adam and me*, Cassie thought. She and Scarlett were linked. They were fated. It explained everything she felt about Scarlett since the moment she'd set eyes on her, how she was willing to go against the whole Circle to defend her and protect her.

If Scarlett saw it, she didn't mention it. She went on talking as usual, while massaging Cassie's hand in her own.

'I'll never forget the day my mother told me I had a sister,' Scarlett said. 'It changed everything for me. I knew one day I'd find you. And see, I was right.'

She waited a moment to read Cassie's expression and then added, 'I don't understand why your mom never told you.'

Cassie suddenly felt herself snap to a new level of awareness. She pulled her hand away. 'Wait a minute. My mother knew about you?'

'Of course she knew.' Scarlett's voice contained the slightest hint of outrage. 'They were all still in New Salem when we were born.'

Cassie thought back to the conversation she recently had with her mother. How she'd looked deep into her eyes and swore she'd told Cassie the whole truth about her father. *I loved that I was all his and he was all mine*, she'd said, but it was a lie. Her mother knew he was with someone else.

The Divide

'How could my mother not have told me I had a sister?' Cassie said aloud. This was a new divide that had sprung up between her and her mother and, at the moment, it felt insurmountable. Her whole childhood and adolescence had been hindered by lies – that truth had come to light when they first moved to New Salem and Cassie learned she was a witch. But she'd come to terms with all the covering up her mother had done in hopes of protecting her. Now it occurred to Cassie that even their more recent conversations had been poisoned by deceit. As of this very moment, her mother was still lying to her. Cassie never felt more estranged from her as she did now.

'She should have told you,' Scarlett said. 'I wonder what else she's kept from you.'

Cassie realised Scarlett was absolutely right. If her mom could lie about the existence of a sibling, she could lie about anything. And if she was keeping secrets, Cassie would, too. She decided right then not to tell her mom anything about meeting Scarlett. Her mother didn't deserve her honesty. She hadn't earned it.

Fortunately, now Cassie had a sister and everything would be different. Everything would be better. If it had to be just the two of them against the rest of the world, so be it. They would remain inseparable, that was the one and only thing Cassie could feel secure about now.

'Scarlett,' she said, feeling her heart overflow with love and affection, 'now that you're here, I finally feel like I'm home.'

'Me, too.' Scarlett's dark eyes shimmered. 'I've never been more sure of anything,' she said. 'This is where I belong.'

Chapter Nineteen

'Do you want a latte or a cappuccino?' Adam asked from the head of the line at the coffee shop counter.

'Surprise me,' Cassie said, and then watched him interact with the barista, placing his order and counting out his money.

Cassie pretended not to know him for a moment and imagined he was a stranger she'd just seen for the first time. She observed his cut jaw and broad shoulders, those auburn curls. *Yes*, she thought to herself. It would be love at first sight all over again.

Things between Cassie and Adam had come around full circle. The past few days since the confrontation with Scarlett at the docks had been romantic and exciting, just like the first days of their relationship. When he kissed her, she shivered with that familiar pleasure and excitement, of loving him so completely with her entire body and soul, and knowing he felt the same.

Since the truth had come out about Scarlett, Adam went back to being Adam, and Cassie went back to being Cassie, but happier and more confident.

Adam returned to their table, setting down an iced mocha topped with whipped cream and a giant chocolate-chip cookie.

'You said to surprise you,' he said.

'You're trying to get me high on sugar.'

'That's how I like you best.' He dipped his finger into the whipped cream for a taste.

Cassie glanced at the door, but the girl entering wasn't Scarlett.

Adam laughed. 'She's only a few minutes late. Relax.'

'I know.' Cassie broke off a hunk of cookie and shoved it into her mouth while Adam took another swipe at the whipped cream. She looked away, not wanting to be caught watching him lick it from his fingers.

'Should I leave you and my iced mocha alone?' she asked.

Adam blushed, pushing the drink closer to Cassie and out of his reach. Then he wiped his mouth with a napkin and tried to be serious. 'I'm so glad for you,' he said.

'Scarlett is pretty amazing. I can totally see how the two of you are related.'

'I tried to tell you,' Cassie said.

'I know. And I've never been happier to admit that I was wrong.'

'Well, you can tell Scarlett that in person, if she ever gets here.' Cassie glanced at the door again and then took a sip of her drink. 'I'm starting to worry that she hasn't shown up yet. I'm going to call her.'

But Scarlett didn't answer her phone and Cassie began to worry even more.

'I have a bad feeling about this,' she said. She knew if she phrased it that way, Adam would take her seriously.

'Then we should go over to the B and B and see if she's there.' Adam stood up, wasting no time.

It was exactly what Cassie wanted him to suggest. Sometimes his predictability was her favourite thing about him.

The bed-and-breakfast where Scarlett was staying was a Georgian building just off Old Town Square. It was one of the most beautiful historical B and Bs in New Salem, owned and operated by an old man whom Cassie knew by sight. She'd grown used to seeing him walking his three Pomeranians around town. A few times, she'd bent down to pet one of the dogs, but she never engaged in much conversation with the old man. It was he who answered the door when they arrived, the dogs yapping and jumping around his feet.

Cassie introduced herself and Adam while the man ordered his dogs to be quiet. Once inside, she stuttered a bit before saying, 'Sorry to bother you, but my sister, Scarlett, is a guest here. We were wondering if she's here.' It was the first time Cassie had ever said those words, *my sister*. It felt exhilarating to say it, but it also felt foreign, as if she were telling a lie.

The man nodded and rubbed at the silver scruff on his chin. 'Yes, yes, Scarlett with the crazy hair,' he said.

'So she's here?' Cassie was momentarily relieved.

'No,' he replied. 'She hasn't been here since yesterday.'

Adam noticed the panic in Cassie's eyes and pressed for more information. 'Are you sure? She never came home last night, not even to sleep?'

'No, she didn't,' the man said, straightening his posture. 'But that's really not your business. A girl has a right to her privacy.' His eyes ricocheted between Adam and Cassie, and then he raised his white eyebrows. 'I'm sorry, but I'm going to have to ask you to leave. I can't give out information on my guests to two strangers, kids or not.'

'Of course,' Adam said. 'We understand. Thank you for your help.' He left a phone number so they could be reached in case Scarlett returned, or if he heard anything of her whereabouts.

Back in the car, Cassie turned to him. 'Now I'm really worried sick. What should we do?'

Adam focused on his driving. 'I think we should give it a little more time,' he said calmly. 'We don't know that she's in trouble. She could just be out and about.'

'Out and about?' Cassie was exasperated. 'If she was just out and about, then she would have shown up at the coffee shop when she was supposed to, or at least answered her phone.'

'Cassie.' Adam chose his words carefully. 'Try to remember that we don't know all that much about Scarlett. She could be off visiting friends and forgot to call you.'

'So you think she'd just stand up her new sister?'

'That's not what I'm saying.'

'You think she's some kind of flake,' Cassie said. 'Just because she's not as uptight as all of you.'

'All of *you*?' Adam gripped the steering wheel tightly and brought the car to a halting stop. 'You mean us, the Circle? Why do you keep insisting on separating yourself from us? I don't understand it, Cassie.'

Cassie was feeling too much all at once to make sense of it. But here they were again, having the same fight they seemed to keep having. She was tired of Adam always trying to reason her out of her true feelings.

'I'm not separating myself,' she said. 'But I don't know what more you need to fully accept Scarlett. She's my sister, Adam.'

'I know,' he said, continuing along Crowhaven Road to Cassie's house. 'I didn't mean anything by suggesting she might not be in trouble. Do you see how quickly you jumped to that conclusion?'

Cassie didn't want to admit it, but she did see that. She was silent until they reached her house. 'I guess I'm just shaken up,' she said finally.

'Let's just give it the night,' Adam said. 'If you still don't hear from her, I promise we'll get the group to look for her in the morning.'

'Okay.' Cassie reached over and gave Adam a kiss on the cheek, but she didn't invite him into her house.

* * *

The Divide

That night Cassie had a dream. One minute she was on a beach, tanning beneath the summer sun with the sound of the ocean and seagulls filling her ears, and the next minute she heard a scream. It was a bloodcurdling scream for help, much like Melanie's scream the night Constance was killed at the festival. In the dream, Cassie opened her eyes and found she was no longer on a sunny beach but in a field or a meadow, at night. And the sky overhead had turned murky, like a polluted body of water.

The scream for help came louder. Cassie thought it was coming from a shadowy house in the distance. It was unmistakably Scarlett's voice, but Cassie couldn't get to it. In fact, she couldn't move at all.

Scarlett! Cassie yelled out, still within the dream. *I can hear you!*

It was all so vivid, Cassie was sure it was real.

The connection worked, Scarlett replied, relieved but still terrified.

Where are you? Cassie asked.

I don't know! The hunters are holding me captive. They're torturing me, studying my powers. Please help me!

Try to stay calm, Cassie said. *Think hard, is there any clue as to where you are?*

Help me, Cassie. Please, hurry. I think they're going to kill me soon.

No! Cassie was losing her. The connection was fading. *Scarlett, can you still hear me? I promise we'll find you, somehow. Scarlett? Hello? Hang on. We'll save you!*

Cassie sat up in bed, startled. She was fully awake now, in her bedroom, alone. Her mahogany furniture stared back at her. She could hear her mother snoring down the hall. All was as it should be.

It was three in the morning. Adam had said to give it the night. But what if Scarlett didn't have till morning? She had to call him.

Shaking, she dialled Adam's number, and the moment he answered, she said, 'Scarlett's been kidnapped.'

Adam sounded groggy and confused. 'What?'

'I dreamed it. But it wasn't a dream. She came to me, Adam. We communicated.'

'Are you sure?'

'I've never been more sure of anything. It's the hunters. They have her.'

'Okay.' Adam cleared his throat. 'I'll put out a call to the others. Where should we meet?'

'Behind my house, out on the bluff. We can't risk waking my mom.'

'Done. I'll be right there.'

'Adam, one more thing.' Cassie could hardly express how thankful she was to have him at a time like this. 'I love you.'

She could almost hear him smile. 'I love you, too,' he said.

Chapter Twenty

Faye, Deborah and Suzan were the last to arrive on the bluff. They staggered towards the others, bleary-eyed and dishevelled, and severely underdressed for the pre-dawn chill. 'They were out having a good time,' Adam said when he saw them coming. 'Looks like they still are.'

'So what's the big emergency?' Faye called out in a voice much too loud. 'It better be good. Do you have any idea what time it is?'

'What's wrong with you?' Melanie asked.

Faye cracked up laughing and patted Melanie on the shoulder. 'You and Laurel aren't the only ones interested in herbology.' She pulled an eyedropper from her pocket. 'Care for a taste? It's all natural.'

Melanie's face hardened. 'This is no time for that,' she said. 'The hunters have Scarlett.'

Faye returned the eyedropper to her pocket. 'I guess that's a no, then.'

Cassie chose to ignore Faye, Deborah and Suzan and only address the others, who were capable of paying attention.

'Scarlett doesn't know where she is,' Cassie said. 'But she's terrified they're going to kill her.'

She went on to describe her dream in vivid detail, how the hunters were holding Scarlett captive, torturing her and studying her powers, and how she begged Cassie to come save her.

'What should we do?' Adam directed the question to Diana, but it was Cassie who answered.

'We need to find out where the hunters are keeping her,' she said. 'We can use the locator spell Constance taught us.'

'Yes!' Faye said, staring up at the moon as if it were speaking to her. 'We're back to using magic!'

'Not so fast.' Diana pursed her lips. 'We have to navigate this very carefully.'

'Buzz-killer,' Faye said.

'What we did on the docks was an exception,' Diana said firmly. 'Using magic still puts us at risk. What if this is a trick to help the hunters figure out who we are?'

'I don't care about that,' Cassie blurted out.

Everyone swung their head in her direction, awestruck by her outburst.

'My sister is in danger,' Cassie continued, refusing to be dismayed. 'It's worth the risk.'

Deborah was the first to break the silence with cackling laughter. 'That's not your call to make, princess.'

Cassie had the urge to scream out again, but she restrained herself and simply said, 'As one of the leaders of this Circle, it is partially my call to make.'

'When are you going to get it?' Faye shouted. 'You don't get to put your own petty needs before the Circle.'

'This is hardly a petty need, Faye,' Cassie said. 'Scarlett is being tortured. They're probably going to kill her.'

'But it's fine with you if we all get killed trying to save her.' Faye turned her back on Cassie dismissively, swatting her pitch-black hair in her direction. 'You're just being selfish.'

'You're one to talk about being selfish,' Cassie shot back. 'Who's more selfish than you?'

'Okay. That's enough.' Diana raised her clear, overpowering voice and called for order.

Adam placed his hand on Cassie's back to calm her. 'There must be a way to perform the locator spell without the hunters tracing it.'

Everyone got quiet for a moment to think, but Cassie couldn't understand all this deliberation. A feeling of heat overcame Cassie, not from outside – the bluff remained cool and breezy – but from deep inside her gut, where a boiling anger seethed.

There's just no way, she thought to herself. She'd have to find Scarlett on her own.

Then Adam shot up from the log he was sitting on. 'We can do it in a crowded place,' he said.

Nobody responded, but Adam had a look of delight across his face, and his breathing was heavy. 'Don't you get it?' he said. 'If we do it in a crowd, the hunters will have a harder time deciphering the source of the magic.'

'That, my friend, is brilliant,' Chris said, giving Adam a high-five.

Melanie's grey eyes widened. 'That totally could work. We could do it during some school event.'

'Under the bleachers,' Laurel called out. 'During the big track meet after school today.'

Cassie threw herself at Adam and wrapped her arms tightly around him. 'This is why I love you,' she said. 'You always have the best ideas.'

Adam's eyes radiated an enchanting blue light. 'Is that

why?' He started laughing and then said, 'Okay, so it's a plan. We do the locator spell this afternoon.'

'We should still put it to a vote,' Diana said brusquely.

Faye smirked. 'Way to kill a moment, D.'

'It's only fair to let everyone have their say on this,' Diana insisted. 'And we should all keep in mind that locating Scarlett is only half of it.' She paused to look at Cassie. 'Deciding what we do from there should be another vote entirely.'

Cassie lashed out, unable to stop herself. 'Do you not understand that they're going to kill her? She's my family. Does that mean nothing to you?'

Diana's lips parted, but no sound escaped. She searched Cassie's eyes as if she were looking for something in them she'd lost.

Cassie's anger wasn't intended solely for Diana, but it may as well have been. She had screamed almost directly into her face. It was no way to behave, but the way Cassie saw it, this wasn't a time for cool analytics and meticulous strategy. Not when Scarlett's life was at stake.

Diana looked at Cassie for another bewildered and speechless moment before turning away. 'We're getting ahead of ourselves,' she said. 'There's no guarantee the locator spell will even work.'

Adam went to Cassie's side and put his arm around her. 'But we're going to try it. Do we all agree?'

There were nods all around.

Adam was so good to her, and it was something that the group was willing to try the spell, but it still wasn't enough to console Cassie. All this voting and planning was wasting too much time. At this rate, they'd never get to Scarlett in time.

Chapter Twenty-One

Cassie went home during lunch to go over all her notes on the locator spell Constance had taught them. Since she'd never actually performed the spell, the details of how it worked were fuzzy in her memory. Her notes went on for a few pages, but as far as Cassie could tell, the spell was intended to locate lost objects. Nowhere had she written about using the spell to find a lost person.

Just then there was a knock on her front door. It was Adam; she should have known.

'I figured I'd find you here,' he said, following Cassie to her bedroom.

'I'm not avoiding the Circle,' she said. 'I wanted to do some research.'

'I know. You're off the hook anyway – everyone went home to gather stuff for the spell.' He plopped down on

Cassie's bed, beckoning her to join him.

Did he really think this was a good time for a make-out session? Cassie sat beside him, holding her notes between them.

'Is this locator spell really going to work on a person?' she asked. 'I didn't realise it's actually a spell to find your missing car keys.'

Adam removed the notes from Cassie's hands and placed them down on the nightstand. 'It might not work,' he said. 'But it's possible it will. These spells can be used to find lost people if those people really want to be found.'

Cassie felt her shoulders settle a bit. There was no question that Scarlett wanted to be found. 'But what if the hunters don't want her to be found?' she asked.

Adam frowned sympathetically. 'That could be a problem. But my guess is the hunters *do* want to be found, because they want us to go to them.' Then his eyes filled with remorse. 'There's a reason they're keeping Scarlett alive, Cassie. Otherwise they would have killed her outright. We will find her. I promise.'

Cassie knew Adam was right. She kissed him softly on the cheek. 'I don't know how I'd get through this without you.'

'Luckily you don't have to,' he said, as he went in for a kiss. For just a moment, the world felt right again.

After school that afternoon, the Circle gathered under the bleachers just before the track-meet finals were set to begin. But Faye was nowhere to be found. Searching the bleachers for her, Cassie and Laurel weren't surprised to find that she wasn't alone.

Crowds had filled in the bleachers on all sides of Faye and Max, but they hadn't noticed. Max was kissing her neck as Faye ran her nails down the length of his torso and tugged at his jeans like a hungry animal.

'So much for her laying off Max,' Laurel said. 'But I guess once the love spell was done, it was done.'

Cassie nodded. 'But Faye's not under a spell, so what's her excuse?'

'She's Faye,' Laurel said.

Cassie noticed Portia walking towards them, or more like marching towards them, wearing a high-collared blouse that was the same shade as her straw-coloured hair.

'Here comes trouble,' Cassie said.

'Will you tell your disgusting friend to go get a room?' Portia shouted. 'This is a track meet, not an R-rated movie.'

Laurel giggled. 'Portia's right. I think they might be scaring the children.'

She turned to Cassie. 'Do you want to go douse them with some ice-water, or should I?'

Portia half smiled. 'Thank you, Laurel. I always knew you were the most reasonable one in your little clique.' Then glancing at Cassie, Portia added, 'Though the bar's been set pretty low.'

'I'll take care of it,' Cassie said, already walking away. She'd take any excuse to escape Portia.

Laurel and Portia continued talking for a few minutes while Cassie did her best to prise Faye away from Max.

'No,' Max whined. 'Where are you taking her?' All the coolness had been sucked out of him.

'Say goodbye, Max,' Cassie insisted. 'Faye has to go now.'

Faye struggled to cop one last feel of him before being hauled away. She grazed her fingers across his chiselled face. 'Be a good boy and stay here,' she said. 'And later you'll get a reward.'

Max's strong features softened with boyish delight. 'Do you promise?' he said.

Faye blew a kiss in response as Cassie dragged her down below the bleachers.

Once they were safely away from him, Cassie shook her head. 'I can hardly believe that's the same Max.'

Faye smiled. 'If you saw him with his shirt off, you'd believe it.'

Below the bleachers, the Circle was almost done preparing the locator spell. Suzan and Sean stuck candles into the ground: one north, one south, one east and one west. Nick ignited the wicks with his brass Zippo.

Melanie tapped Cassie on the shoulder. 'Excuse me,' she said, bumping her to the side. 'I've got censers to light.'

'Won't they smell the incense?' Cassie asked, referring to the bleacher crowd above.

'No,' Melanie replied, while clearing the ground's energy. 'It's only jasmine. If anything, they'll think someone's smoking something.'

'Is everybody ready to begin?' Diana called out, eyeing Cassie.

She'd taken Cassie aside after chemistry class to hash out what happened at their morning meeting. She tried to explain her position, that she wished to save Scarlett as much as Cassie did, but she had to balance that wish with her responsibility to the Circle. *It isn't personal*, she'd said.

Cassie assured Diana she understood. But it *was* personal. That's what nobody seemed to recognise. To Cassie this was all very personal.

The sound of their schoolmates cheering above them indicated the track meet had begun.

'We're ready as we'll ever be,' Laurel said.

The group sat in a circle surrounding the candles as Diana instructed them to do. Then Diana placed a goblet of water within the circle.

'Everyone invoke the element of Water,' she said.

Cassie gazed into the goblet, imagining it contained the whole ocean, so blue and cold and deep that if she tried to stick her fingers inside it to reach its bottom, she never would.

'Power of Water, I beseech you,' Diana said. And then, together as a group, the Circle softly repeated the incantation four times.

> *That which is lost shall now be found*
> *Hiding places come unbound*

They stared into the goblet as Diana called out, 'Let the water show the location of Scarlett.'

At first there was nothing, just some ordinary water

pooled in a fancy glass. The crowd above their heads cheered and rose to their feet, and the water stirred. It took a few seconds for it to go still again, but when it did, Cassie noticed her own reflection in the water becoming more pronounced. The shape of her own face, her round eyes and pouting mouth, sharpened to a pristine clarity. How frightened she looked to herself, how desperate. But soon that faded away and a new image emerged, with equal clarity. It was a broken-down house – the same house as the one in her dream, except now she could really see it, not just sense it.

It was a rickety beach cottage, in what Cassie recognised as the classic Cape Cod style. It sat near the end of a long, desolate, sandy lane, with a large body of water on one side and tidal marshes on the other.

I know this place, Cassie thought, but in the next moment, the image transformed into something else.

What was it?

The image was forming slowly, but she could swear it was a loaf of bread. Then the loaf separated into slices. Maybe she was just hungry, because as quickly as that image formed, it re-shaped into something else: It was the face of a man who appeared to be from the 1800s. He had bushy eyebrows and a thick moustache and wore a high collar. Cassie was sure she recognised this man, too, but from where?

And then, finally, the image changed one last time – to a number. It flashed for only a second, almost too quickly to catch, but it was *48*. It appeared to Cassie like a numbered ball plucked from a lottery. Then the water blackened and became still.

'I think Scarlett's in Cape Cod,' Cassie said, looking to the others for confirmation.

'Yes,' Adam agreed. 'In the town of Sandwich. It's in the north-west corner of the Cape.'

Cassie laughed to herself. Of course. Why hadn't she figured that out? 'But who was that man?' she asked.

'I know I've seen him before,' Diana said.

And then it was Melanie's turn to have a laugh. 'I just read *The Scarlet Letter*,' she said. 'That was Nathaniel Hawthorne.'

'It was probably a clue to a street name,' Laurel suggested. 'Lots of the streets are named after old authors around there.'

'Forty-eight,' Adam said, typing it into his phone. 'Forty-eight Hawthorne Street, that's where she is.'

'Well, what are we standing around for?' Nick said. 'Let's go get her.'

'We can't,' Diana said firmly. 'Cape Cod is outside the realm of the protective spell. It's too dangerous.'

Melanie, sensing that Cassie was about to explode, backed Diana up. 'We'll need all the power we can get if we have a chance at defeating the hunters,' she said. 'We should wait to battle them here in New Salem, under the guard of the protection spell.'

'I'm done waiting,' Cassie said. 'We can't count on the hunters sparing Scarlett for long.'

Before anyone had the chance to respond, there was a spine-chilling scream from the bleachers overhead. It immediately registered that this was not the right kind of scream to hear at a track meet. It was a grisly sound, pain and shock and horror all wrapped into one. It sounded like death.

Cassie and the others hurried out to see what happened, but it was complete havoc when they emerged. They strived to see over the mad crowd of panic-stricken students and frantic teachers and parents.

'There's a student down, on the bleachers,' Adam said.

Cassie caught sight of a head of straw-coloured hair and instantly knew who it was. It was Portia Bainbridge. And she was lying right above where the Circle did their spell.

'She collapsed,' someone from the track team said.

Laurel elbowed through the crowd to see if Portia was still alive. She knelt over her body, calling her name, and checked for a pulse. But it was no use.

Portia was gone – as lifelessly stiff as Constance had been on the ground the night of the spring festival. And what was worse, what Cassie wished more than anything she hadn't seen, was the faint glimmer of the hunter symbol on Portia's shirt, just over the place where her heart would have been beating.

Cassie didn't need to ask the others if they could also see it this time. She knew by their fright-stricken faces that they could.

'We need to get out of here,' Melanie said, ghost-faced.

'Now,' Diana commanded. 'Everyone to my house.'

Scattered around Diana's living room, the Circle tried to regroup. But they were reeling from Portia's shocking death and their own near miss.

Adam was walking in figure eights upon the hooked rug, gnawing on his fingernails. 'Don't you see what this means?' he said. 'The hunters killed a human, thinking the source of the magic was coming from her. So they don't know who the witches are yet.'

'They still don't know it's us,' Faye echoed from where she was lounging on Diana's sofa. 'After all this time. I told you so.' There was a hint of triumph in her voice.

Laurel cringed at Faye's insensitivity. 'But that was a huge price to find that out, don't you think? Portia's dead.'

'Ah yes, more Outsider blood on our hands,' Faye said mockingly.

Suzan unwrapped a Twinkie she had buried in her purse and emotionally bit off its top.

With her mouth full she mumbled, 'I was finally starting to not hate Portia, too. And then we go and get her killed.'

'It wasn't our fault,' Deborah said. 'There was no way we could have known that would happen.'

Melanie disagreed. 'We knew doing a spell as powerful as that was a risk, and we willingly took that risk. Portia would still be alive if we hadn't.'

Until now Cassie had remained silent. Of course she felt responsible for what happened to Portia, but there wasn't time to dwell on it at the moment. She took control of the floor, hoping to channel the group's fear and anger, and even their guilt, towards the task at hand.

'I'm as rattled as the rest of you,' Cassie announced.

'This proves the hunters are strong and getting closer. And Scarlett is still being held hostage and tortured in a shack on Cape Cod as we speak. We have to act fast before she reaches the same fate as Portia.'

Diana began shaking her head before Cassie had even finished her sentence. 'I'm sorry, Cassie, but we just can't risk it. We'll figure out another way.'

Melanie jumped right in to aid Diana in shutting Cassie down. 'We can't mess with these hunters. Look at what they're capable of.'

Faye appeared to be utterly enjoying herself. What was it that charged her up? Was it the brutal loss of human life, the fractioning of the group or everyone turning on Cassie?

She sat upright from her lounging position on the sofa. 'You had to know there was no way we would step right into the hunters' hands, right?' She narrowed her snakelike eyes at Cassie. 'Not with this group of cowards, anyway.'

Nick rose up from his chair. 'Shouldn't we put it to a vote?'

'No.' Faye laughed. 'It's called veto power. Right, D?'

Diana looked down at her thin hands. 'It's called an executive decision.'

'We can't go after the hunters in Cape Cod,' Adam said. 'But what if we try to lure them back here to New Salem?'

'There's no time for that!' Cassie lost her patience.

Chris Henderson shot up and went to Nick's side. 'We should vote. Like we always do.'

'I agree.' Doug joined his brother and Nick in their small insurrection. 'Since when did you all become fascists? I say we go rescue Scarlett.' Then directly to Cassie he said, 'I know what it's like to lose a sister. You shouldn't have to.'

'And I trust Cassie's judgement,' Nick called out. His jaw was tight, but his eyes were full of emotion. 'I'm willing to take the risk.'

Cassie's heart was confused. How could her soulmate not understand her the way Nick sometimes did? Adam was standing there now, stubborn and overly protective, shaking his head no while Nick was willing to do whatever it took to support Cassie and rescue Scarlett.

'It's not going to happen, boys,' Faye said maliciously.

'We have the right to vote on it,' Nick insisted, with Chris and Doug growing visibly more restless at his side.

But even if they voted, it was clear who would win. After everything they'd been through, Scarlett was still an Outsider to them. They would do anything to save

Melanie's great-aunt, but when Cassie's own sister was in trouble, and they had a way to save her, they refused.

'Fine.' Diana appeared flustered and a little annoyed by this mutiny. 'We'll vote. But the decision is the final decision for the Circle. And let me just remind you that –'

'Save your energy.' Cassie cut Diana off. 'I don't need your vote. I don't need any of you.' She walked away, leaving a fracture in the Circle as she went.

Chapter Twenty-Two

Cassie lay awake staring up at the canopy cascading down from her four-poster bed. She observed the sun reflecting off the pewter candlesticks upon the mantel and off the china clock on the opposite wall. At times she still felt like a stranger in this room, as if she were at an extended slumber party at some other girl's house.

When Cassie didn't get out of bed at her regular time, her mother knocked on her door gently with her knuckles.

'You're going to be late for school,' her mother said, letting herself into the light-filled room.

Cassie didn't bother to say she didn't feel well. She didn't bother to speak at all. In fact, she was nearly catatonic in her motionless silence.

'You don't look so good,' her mother said, squinting with concern. 'Are you sick?'

Cassie had been avoiding her mother since the night she found out she had a sister. She knew if she confronted her about it, her mother would only try to explain it away like she did everything else. So instead, Cassie held the secret close to her chest, like a concealed weapon.

Her mother felt her forehead. Fretfully, she examined Cassie's eyes and the flushness of her skin. 'I don't think you're running a temperature,' she said.

Her long dark hair, pulled back from her face, made her appear even paler and thinner than usual, and Cassie worried that her mother was actually the one who wasn't well.

But as much as Cassie wanted to open up to her mother and tell her everything that was going on, she couldn't. She wasn't ready to forgive her yet.

'I'm not going to school today,' Cassie said bluntly, making it clear she was in no way asking permission to stay home.

But her mother didn't argue. 'I'll make you a hot cup of tea,' she said.

'I don't want any tea.'

'Okay then, no tea.' She retrieved an extra blanket from the mahogany chest in the corner, shook it out and covered Cassie with it lovingly. 'Is everything all right,

Cassie? Are you angry at me about something?'

Cassie turned onto her side, away from her mother. 'I'm not angry,' she said to the window. 'I'm tired. Will you close the door on your way out?'

Her mother made no sound for a few seconds, but Cassie could sense her deliberating, whether she should push her daughter to talk to her when she knew something was wrong or let it go and give her the space she asked for.

'Please,' Cassie said, to help her along. 'Can you just go and let me rest?'

Her mother inhaled and then exhaled deeply. It was the sound of resignation. 'Okay,' she said. 'Let me know if you need anything. I'll make some soup for lunch later.' She made her way out of the room without another word.

Cassie couldn't have felt more alone once the door clicked shut. Her mom was a stranger to her and, as if that weren't enough, Adam had sided against her at their last meeting, and Diana felt like more of an enemy than a friend. Cassie had no one to turn to.

She got out of bed and went to the window. The sight of the jewel-blue water always soothed her, but it looked cool and lonely to her today.

The Divide

I have to find some way to save Scarlett, Cassie thought. *No matter what it takes.*

What good was it being a witch if Cassie couldn't use her powers? Then again, how much power did she have without the full Circle behind her?

A shiver ran up her spine as she stared out at the ocean, but no answers came to her. She perceived the immeasurable span of the water and its waves, but her internal rhythm didn't synch to it the way it usually did. For once, it didn't appear to her that the sky and sea were waiting, watching and listening to her.

She began to feel feverish, achy and clammy. *You're not actually sick,* she told herself, but she still returned to bed and buried herself deep within her covers. Minutes passed, maybe an hour, but she couldn't rest. Every time she drifted toward a loose, mind-numbing sleep, she'd startle awake. How could she allow herself to rest at a time like this?

Her Book of Shadows was in arm's reach within her nightstand drawer. She pulled it out and paged through it, searching for some hint or clue as to what to do next. But she knew deep down there were no magical short-cuts. She would have to go to Cape Cod and battle the hunters herself. It was the only way. She could die trying, and she knew it, but she couldn't think of a better reason to die.

Her thoughts were interrupted then by another knock at her bedroom door, this time louder and less gentle.

'Mom, I'm sleeping,' she called out.

'It's Adam,' said the voice behind the door.

Cassie didn't tell him to come in, but he turned the knob and opened the door anyway. 'Your mom said you weren't feeling well,' he said, closing the door behind him.

Cassie watched him with indifference. 'I'm fine,' she said.

He kicked off his shoes and sat on the bed beside her. Something glistened in his eyes that made Cassie realise he was going to try to sweet talk her.

'I don't recall telling you to make yourself comfortable,' she said.

He didn't flinch. 'I get it, Cassie. You're angry with me. But please hear me out.'

Cassie made no reply.

Adam took that as his cue to continue. 'You know I'm always on your side,' he said. 'And I want to save Scarlett just as much as you do. We all do.'

'Then there shouldn't be a problem,' Cassie said. 'We all want the same thing.'

Adam furrowed his brow. 'I wasn't finished,' he said. 'I want to save Scarlett, but I'm worried about how this is playing out. And I don't want you, or any of us, to get hurt.'

'This is beginning to sound like a broken record, Adam. All anyone talks about is how dangerous everything is, how we can't perform magic, how we can't go after the hunters. I'm beginning to think Faye is right. This Circle is a bunch of cowards.'

Adam pitched forward slightly, as if Cassie had socked him in the gut. 'I'm not a coward,' he said.

Prove it, she wanted to say, but she felt a spasm of self-reproach. Battering Adam would get her nowhere. There would be no convincing him to see this her way.

'I'm not a coward,' Adam said again, tightly, and for a moment Cassie glimpsed something in him that she found frightening. A commanding power that always lay dormant inside him. If only she could harness that power to work for her rather than against her on this.

Cassie knew deep within her soul how powerful the Circle actually was when they worked together. They didn't need to rely on a protection spell to keep them safe. Why couldn't Adam see that?

'I can't talk about this with you now,' Cassie said. 'I

need some time to myself. To think.'

Adam stood up. His eyes turned as dark as the sky in a storm. 'I love you,' he said. 'And if you have to be upset with me in order to prove that love, that's fine. But I'm not willing to lose you.'

He put his hands on his hips. The sun glimmering through the window brought out all the different colours in his hair, the shining waves of red mixed with brown and gold.

'If time is what you want, okay,' he said. 'I'll be here when you're ready. But I have one request.'

He paused to make sure Cassie was listening carefully to him.

'What's your request?' she asked, still not returning his gaze.

'Don't do anything rash without talking to the Circle first.'

Cassie buckled. That wasn't exactly a fair thing to ask of her.

'Promise me,' he said.

She made the mistake then of looking into Adam's pained, loving eyes. He wasn't a coward. He was a good, brave soul, and he always wanted the best for everyone.

'Please,' he said. 'Don't do anything reckless.'

The Divide

Cassie was no less angry with him than she was when he arrived, but she also loved him with all her heart. And she was powerless against the urge to put his troubled mind at ease. 'I promise,' she said.

But she knew it was a promise she probably couldn't keep.

Chapter Twenty-Three

Darkness for miles, that was all Cassie could see. A red-toned darkness like the insides of her own eyelids, but her eyes were wide open. She sensed the ramshackle house far out in the distance, hidden within the blackened night. She called out, *Scarlett!*

Scarlett didn't come to Cassie in this dream – Cassie went to her. She forced her way through the pitch-black night as if blind and mad, hollering Scarlett's name. It was like travelling through outer space in a starless universe, but with persistence Cassie hit upon what she was searching for. The house. And through the rickety door of the house, Cassie discovered Scarlett. She was bound at the wrists and ankles to a splintered wooden post and she was screaming.

They were whipping her. Whoever they were. Cassie

tried to make out the hunters' faces, but she couldn't. They didn't have faces; they were formless black entities like ghosts. She could only sense their trembling dark souls and how they were frightened to the point of brutality. It was their fear driving them, fear of the unknown, of the supernatural, of witchcraft. Like Holy War soldiers, their faith in their own righteousness was unbreakable and their capacity for violence against their enemies was extreme. They whipped Scarlett mercilessly over and over again, unaffected by her screams.

Cassie wondered why the hunters didn't tape Scarlett's mouth shut, to quiet her. And then the thought occurred to her like a light being switched on. The hunters wanted Scarlett to talk, to spill information – not only the secrets of her magic, Cassie realised, but the secrets of the Circle, who they were and where to find them. Scarlett cried and shrieked and spat at the shapeless hunters, but no words escaped her bruised mouth. Was she bearing all this pain to protect the Circle? And to protect Cassie?

Her beaten body hung from the wooden post limp and wilted like a dying flower. Her face was a mess of blood and dirt, and one of her eyes had swelled completely shut. Her damp red hair dripped like blood down her bony shoulders. She'd been stripped almost nude; her torso and legs were streaked with lash marks and purple welts. How much longer could she possibly take such abuse?

Like in the last dream she'd had, Cassie couldn't move. Her feet were frozen in place at the doorway – from where she could see Scarlett but wasn't sure if Scarlett could see her. She called out to her from where she stood.

Scarlett, I know where you are, she said. *And I'll be there soon. I promise.*

With that, she jolted awake.

My sister, Cassie thought, *my poor, dear sister*. She'd rather Scarlett give the hunters what they wanted, to tell them the entire truth about the Circle, if it meant they'd release her alive. Better that than seeing her die to protect them. Scarlett had come to New Salem to seek out the safety of the Circle, not the other way around. How had the situation come to this?

But Scarlett was still alive, that much Cassie was sure of. And as long as she was still alive, there was still time to rescue her. Maybe if the Circle understood that Scarlett was being tortured for protecting them, they'd consider rescuing her a little more seriously. Maybe they'd finally accept her as one of their own.

And then there was a piercingly loud sound in Cassie's

ear. She looked over at her nightstand and realised her phone was ringing, but who could be calling at this time of night?

'Hello?' Cassie answered cautiously, half believing it was going to be one of the ancient witch hunters from her dream on the other end of the line. But the scratchy voice that apologized for waking her belonged to Deborah.

'What's happened?' Cassie knew if Deborah was calling her in the middle of the night that someone was either hurt or dead, possibly both.

'Someone set Laurel's lawn on fire,' Deborah said. 'Burning in the shape of the hunter symbol.'

If Cassie hadn't just woken from a nightmare, she would have sworn she'd just entered one.

'Laurel's been marked,' Deborah added, in case Cassie didn't comprehend the full magnitude of the situation.

Cassie suddenly felt like she was suffocating, like one of the hunters from her nightmare had grabbed hold of her neck and was squeezing the breath out of her.

'Cassie?' Deborah said. 'Are you okay?'

Cassie coughed. Laurel. Of all people to be marked, they'd gotten to sweet, peace-loving Laurel. How could this be happening?

'I'm just shocked,' Cassie said. 'Go on.'

Deborah resumed speaking in her gravelly whisper. 'So we're going to have a Circle meeting early tomorrow before school. To figure out what to do.'

'Of course,' Cassie said. 'I'll be there.'

'We're meeting at Diana's. At six-thirty a.m.'

'Okay.' Cassie felt shaky and weird. Her voice didn't come out sounding like her own. Those invisible hands were still squeezing her throat closed, making it hard for her to breathe. 'Is Laurel all right?' she managed to ask.

But the phone clicked. Deborah had already hung up. It struck Cassie as strange that of all the Circle members who could have called her with this news, it was Deborah who did it. Not Adam or Diana.

Careful not to wake her mother, Cassie got out of bed, slipped on her sneakers and wrapped her jacket around her shoulders. Then she unlatched the front door and slinked out to the edge of their property. From high up on the bluff she had a long view of the whole block, every old house on crooked Crowhaven Road – the ones in good repair as well as the ones that looked as if they might tip over into splintering timbers in a strong wind.

Cassie strained her eyes to see far out. First, she saw that the fire had been extinguished, but she could still smell the remnants of smoke and burned grass in the air.

And then she noticed two bodies moving around in the dark, along the outskirts of the lawn. It was difficult to make out who it was through the lingering smoke. Cassie squinted her eyes, but it was no use. She considered taking the walk down. It had to be someone in the Circle. But then the bodies began moving closer, and Cassie recognised who it was. It was Adam and Diana.

Diana's long blonde hair shined beneath the streetlights as she walked, closely and carefully with Adam, towards her house.

Cassie felt a pang of resentment. They were both up and out, together. And neither of them took the time to call Cassie themselves.

How had she drifted so far from the two most important people in her life?

Cassie turned around and went home with an emptiness in her stomach. She tiptoed across the living room floor, back to her bedroom and gently closed the door. Then she kicked off her shoes and climbed into bed, sorry she'd ever left it in the first place.

She could guess what they were doing. They were planning, strategising and plotting the meeting that would happen in a few hours. That was just who they were and how they would always be. The brave knight and the high priestess, ever vigilant. They were the real influence behind the group, no matter who was called leader or who wore the Tools.

Adam may have been Cassie's soulmate, but there would always be the Circle. And the Circle, if represented by one person, would be Diana. Not for one second did Cassie suspect that Adam was cheating on her with Diana. He didn't have to. What he shared with Diana was something above and beyond cheating.

Cassie stared up at her ceiling, sleepless. Let them strategise. Cassie was done waiting on the sidelines. She would go to rescue Scarlett herself and destroy the hunters before they marked anyone else – and before they had the opportunity to kill Laurel.

But Cassie knew she'd need two things if she was going to fight the hunters by herself: the diadem and garter from Diana and Faye.

Chapter Twenty-Four

The next morning, Cassie arrived at Diana's house with coffee and fresh muffins. Diana looked a little unsteady accepting the bag of baked goods from Cassie, unsure of what to make of her kind gesture. Since they'd last disagreed and Cassie stormed out of their Circle meeting, they'd avoided each other. So it was only fair for Diana to be a little suspicious of such an abrupt and dramatic change of heart.

'Will you join me for a moment at the kitchen table before the others arrive?' Diana asked Cassie.

Cassie sat, pulled one of the coffees closer to her and listened.

Diana nibbled on the end of a corn muffin. 'I was up all night researching spells to reverse a mark,' she said. 'To save Laurel.'

'And?'

'Nothing has been perfect yet, but it's promising. I'm hoping to figure out a way of combining an uncrossing spell with a healing spell.'

All Cassie could think about was the diadem, but she forced herself to nod encouragingly at Diana.

'Let me know if there's anything I can do to help,' Cassie said. She knew she needed to give Diana more to regain her trust.

'I know I've been acting a bit heated lately,' Cassie continued. 'And I shouldn't have walked out of the last meeting that way, when it's so important for us to stick together.'

Diana's eyebrows lifted and Cassie could sense her heart filling with hope.

'And I want to help keep the Circle together, at its strongest,' Cassie said. 'I truly believe that together we are strong enough to defeat the hunters.'

Diana tilted her chin at Cassie just as Adam appeared at her side door.

The sight of Cassie made his tense, watchful face loosen. Then his eyes briefly met Diana's and a flicker of understanding passed between them.

'I hope I'm not interrupting,' Adam said. 'But I have to

admit, it's nice to see you two talking.'

Diana smiled at Adam, fully convinced the air between her and Cassie had been cleared. She gave up on her muffin and reached for Cassie's hand.

'I'm so glad you've come around,' she said. 'We're going to go after these hunters here on our own turf.' Her emerald eyes pooled with tears. 'That's how I can be sure *my* sister is safe.'

Adam joined them at the table, grabbing a coffee, not wanting to be left out of their conversation. 'And remember, Cassie,' he said, 'Scarlett is a powerful witch, as powerful as you. Maybe even more powerful.' He stirred his coffee. 'You have to trust that she can take care of herself.'

Soon the rest of the group began trickling in. Deborah arrived with Melanie and a panicked Laurel. Nick, looking icily handsome, stepped in behind her. They were followed by Chris and Doug, and a slinking, half-asleep Sean. Finally, Faye arrived with Suzan, who nearly knocked her over in a rush towards the plate of muffins.

For a few minutes, everyone fussed around the kitchen table, drinking and eating. The group's chatty conversation had a different quality than usual. Cassie felt a chill coming off them, a new kind of fear. And she sensed a darkness within herself, as if with this latest threat she'd been pushed farther out to the periphery of the group for good.

It was easy for Cassie to slip away unnoticed. She swiftly grabbed her purse and made her way to the bathroom without anyone missing a beat. Then she kept walking. She knew the diadem was hidden in Diana's room. All she had to do was find it. And the door to Diana's room was open, practically inviting her inside.

She paused at the threshold. There was no undoing this once she stepped inside. She had to be sure she was willing to suffer the consequences later on. But remembering her nightmares and the sound of Scarlett screaming was all it took to convince her to take that critical step through the doorway.

Cassie had grown so accustomed to the elegance of Diana's room. At one time it struck her as an oddly adult room for a teenager to have, but today it seemed perfect for Diana.

Now, if she were Diana, where would she have hidden the diadem?

Cassie let her eyes hover around the room and pass over each piece of antique-looking furniture. She gazed at the window seat and the many hanging prisms in front of it. The morning sun struck them full on, reflecting tiny rainbows on the opposite side of the room. Bursts of multicoloured light swayed back and forth upon the goddess prints above Diana's bed.

Cassie grinned. The goddess prints. She knew Diana, her sworn sister, so well; she didn't even need to resort to magic to realise exactly where the diadem was hidden.

There were six prints in all. Five of them were similar, black-and-white and slightly old-fashioned. They were the Greek goddesses Aphrodite, the goddess of love; Artemis, the huntress; Hera, the queen of the gods; Athena, the goddess of wisdom; and Persephone, the goddess of all growing things. But the last print was different from the others. It was in colour, and was larger and more modern. It was a young woman beneath a starry sky, with a crescent moon shining down on her long, flowing hair. It was the goddess Diana. And she wore the same white garment Diana wore at Circle meetings as well as a garter on her thigh and a silver cuff-bracelet on her upper arm. And, most importantly, on her head was a thin circlet with a crescent moon, horns upward. The diadem.

Of course, Cassie thought. It was almost too obvious.

Cassie rested her hand against the print and then

gently lifted it up off the wall. Just as she suspected, the wall behind the frame had been hollowed out, and there it was. Resting within that secret cave of torn plaster and drywall was a silver document box.

Cassie reached for it hungrily and unsealed its top. And there, quietly seated within the confines of that silver box, was the shimmering diadem in all its glory.

Quickly Cassie shoved the diadem deep into her bag and replaced the box snugly back into the wall. She rehung the print over the hole and straightened it to just the way she'd found it.

The entire terrible act took less than five minutes to complete. The antique furniture still sat in place and the prisms still shot colourful rainbows around the room. All appeared just as she'd found it. But the diadem in her bag felt charged – it felt alive. She could sense its power quaking at her side.

Cassie returned to the group innocently, shoving her bag onto the seat of one of the kitchen chairs and then pushing it beneath the table. The group had relocated to the living room, where they were sprawled across the couch and the floor, surrounding the centre table. Everyone was looking at Cassie now and they were peculiarly silent.

Cassie held her breath. Perhaps she'd taken longer than she thought.

'What happened, did you fall in?' Doug Henderson called out, and everyone laughed.

'Sorry.' Cassie exhaled with relief. 'I was fixing my make-up.'

Adam scolded Doug with his eyes and then invited Cassie to sit beside him on the couch. The meeting was about to begin.

Cassie smiled harmlessly and went to Adam. She took his warm strong hand in hers and waited for Diana to rise and begin speaking. She felt not a single ounce of guilt for what she'd just done. This was so unlike her, but she knew that if she were in danger, Scarlett would do the same for her. The group would understand once it was all over, once she single-handedly rescued Scarlett and defeated the hunters with the power of the Master Tools at her command. Then they would see that she was right all along, and that even her stealing the Master Tools from her fellow leaders was a necessary evil. A *necessary evil*, that was a concept Cassie had never really thought about before, but that had to be what this was.

She glanced over at her bag in the kitchen and could swear there was an energy surrounding it, a force of

white strength and vigour. She hoped no one else noticed.
All she needed to do now was get the garter from Faye.

Chapter Twenty-Five

Some would say sneaking around outside Faye Chamberlain's house in the middle of the night was a death wish, and they would be correct. But Cassie had come too far at this point to back down now; plus she'd come prepared. She'd spent the whole day studying her Book of Shadows, memorising every spell her mind could hold that might help her get through this covert mission undetected.

Faye had way too much fun with spells, so there was no way the garter was going to be left unguarded. Traceable or not, magic was the only way Cassie would be able to get her hands on it. But first she had to find it.

Cassie was familiar with how to break into Faye's house through the basement. All she had to do was unhook the latch of the wooden cellar door in the back yard and slip down to the cement floor below – the same way she knew Faye snuck in and out during all hours of the night.

Once inside, Cassie looked around. The basement was dark and mouldy, crowded with dusty crates and damp cardboard boxes. It crossed Cassie's mind that if Faye had snuck out tonight and returned through the cellar door behind her, she would be caught. And to be caught by Faye was as good as being destroyed by Faye. Cassie glanced behind her to the closed door and then cautiously around the musty room. She had to keep going; there was no turning back now, regardless of the risk. Before she allowed her fear to get the better of her, she decided to try a summoning spell for the garter.

Grasping the pendant of pink quartz around her neck, Cassie whispered the incantation she'd memorised from her Book of Shadows, modifying it for her current purpose.

> Lost for now
> Soon to be found
> Ancient garter come unbound

Nothing happened at first, but she waited patiently, circled the room and repeated the words again.

No luck. And she felt nothing. So she decided to try something stronger. It was also a summoning spell, but her Book of Shadows said this spell could track down the energy of an object rather than simply the physical object itself.

For this spell Cassie had to focus extra hard. She closed her eyes and breathed deeply until she'd centred herself to a meditative state. It took a few minutes, but soon her breathing took on a rhythm like a heartbeat. She let herself become immersed in this rhythm until she was overcome with the feeling that she controlled it, as if the pulse of life itself were under her command. When the words came, they started from deep within her belly.

> *Guiding Spirits, I ask your charity*
> *Lend me your focus and your clarity*
> *Ancient garter, I summon thee*
> *Black to white, dark to light*
> *Show me your precious energy*

Cassie opened her eyes to find a glowing aquamarine light in front of her. It hovered, waiting for her to observe it, and then soared forward through the air, leaving a trail in its wake like a comet tail.

Now this was what Cassie always imagined magic to look and feel like. She followed the aquamarine trail around the basement until it led her to the storage space beneath the stairs.

Cassie was elated. This had to be the place.

And then she heard something – footsteps above her head. She lost her breath and felt her whole body stiffen while she listened for the footsteps again. She stood perfectly still, scoping the basement's corners for possible hiding spots. Then she heard the sound again and realised it was only the wind from outside blowing against the wooden door. It was just a false alarm, thank goodness, but it was enough to break her concentration. The aquamarine light flickered.

The space under the stairs was low and narrow and packed full with boxes. Cassie brushed her hands over a few of their damp surfaces to see if she felt any vibes coming from one over another. Careful not to make too much noise, she sorted through them until she noticed one box with a faint design on its side – a swirl similar to a Celtic knot. Hurriedly, Cassie lifted its flap and looked inside. There she found another box. A steel document box. In her excitement, she reached for it without thinking. It sparked at her touch, singeing the skin of her fingers.

Of course Faye had it guarded. Cassie dug into her pocket and retrieved the obsidian crystal she'd brought from home. Black like lava with sharp edges, the rock was the size of her hand and could easily be used as a weapon. But Cassie brought it for its ability to purify dark matter. She glided the crystal over and around the steel box to disable Faye's spell while whispering the words she'd memorised: 'Darkness be gone, no shields are needed, purity enters and leaves here unhindered.'

And it worked. When Cassie tapped the box with her fingertip a second time to see if it drew a spark, it was cool and quiet to her touch. Confidently now, she popped the lid off the top of the metal box.

But she didn't find the garter inside. Instead she found a note scrawled in blood-red ink that said, *Nice try*.

Cassie slammed the box closed, furious. Typical Faye. Cassie was going to have to get crafty if she were to pull this off. She had to think like Faye.

Faye was . . . what? Faye was . . . possessive, to say the least. She would trust only herself as the garter's security system. She must be keeping it close by. In fact, it probably never left her sight.

Suddenly Cassie knew, beyond any shadow of a doubt, what she had to do next. She had to go to Faye's room, where she was sleeping, and find the garter there. That was the only place it could be, where Faye could protect it even as she slept.

Now Cassie wished Faye *had* snuck out tonight, leaving her room empty. But Cassie knew it was time to act, not think. A silence spell would help with getting upstairs.

'From my chin to my toes, a mute silence grows.' Cassie slid her fingers from her mouth down the length of her torso, across her arms and legs, all the way to her feet, feeling every inch of her go soundless beneath her touch. When she stepped forward, the feeling of her shoe touching the floor remained the same, but not a single hint of noise accompanied it. Even when she jumped up and down, no sound escaped from the motion. It was eerie but amazing.

Like a stealthy thief in the night, she made her way up the main staircase, through the lavish living room, to Faye's bedroom door. She turned the knob and pushed the door open with assurance.

The room looked the same as Cassie remembered it, but darker. Moonlight shone in from the wide window, but it was still difficult to see, and Cassie couldn't risk waking Faye with the beam of her flashlight. There were many red candles strewn about, but of course they were all unlit. Cassie waited a few seconds to let her eyes adjust and then words she hadn't known before came to her.

By the power of the sun, make the dark become light
And give me sight to see at night

Suddenly, Cassie could see in the dark as if she'd slipped on night-vision goggles. And there Faye was, sleeping, snoring ever so softly. For a split second, Cassie felt a tenderness towards her – it was by far the most peaceful Cassie had ever seen Faye. She looked almost childlike, serenely curled up in her huge bed, surrounded by soft cushions and embroidered pillows. Her tangled, pitch-black hair cascaded down in long full curls, framing her face in such a way that Cassie could hardly remember what it was that made Faye so scary in her waking hours.

But Cassie shook herself from the notion. She knew she was in a dangerous place, and Faye was like a sleeping dragon protecting a jewel. One false move and Cassie would be—

Before she could even finish her thought, the dust ruffle on the bed stirred and out poked the head of an orange cat, followed by a grey one.

Cassie had forgotten about Faye's bloodsucking

kittens. They were fully grown cats now. No doubt with sharper teeth and claws than the last time Cassie encountered them. Cassie stood very still and watched the creatures slink out from beneath the bed. She may have been silent, but the cats could still see her and smell her. They sniffed at her toes, purring. The orange one pawed up her leg to the knee and then hissed. Then the grey one clawed at her foot and took a vicious swipe at the skin of her ankle.

Glancing at Faye, she kicked the grey cat from her right foot, sending it tumbling across the carpet. But that only seemed to make the orange one angrier. From where it was perched with both paws upon Cassie's left knee, it leaped for her face, swiping its sharp claws at her cheek.

No! Cassie screamed, but her voice made no sound. With a swift motion of defence, she grabbed the cat by the scruff of its neck. It cut at her wrist with its claws and bit through the skin of her hand. Blood dripped down from her fingers to the floor.

She tossed the orange cat out of the room, closing the door in its face before it could take another lunge at her. Meanwhile, the grey cat had jumped up on the bed, needling at Faye's neck, trying to stir her awake.

'Ouch!' Faye cried.

And with the speed of a cat herself, Cassie bolted for Faye's closet, soundlessly shutting herself inside before Faye could detect her.

'Ow – what has gotten into you?' Faye, fully awake now, scolded the grey cat.

Out of habit, Cassie held her breath and closed her eyes from inside the closet.

Faye got quiet again, but Cassie could hear the rustling of bedsheets. She was sure Faye sensed something was amiss. Explanations and apologies raced through her mind. If only she knew a spell to make herself invisible. That was the only thing that could save her now if Faye opened the closet door.

But then Faye chuckled absent-mindedly. 'That's better,' she said. 'Now let Mama get her beauty rest. You can sleep up here with me tonight if you promise to be good.'

Cassie exhaled. That was too close. But when she reopened her eyes, the closet appeared different. An unusual aquamarine light was radiating from a piece of clothing hanging in the closet.

The location spell had worked, and it was still working for her. The glowing light was hovering just inside Faye's favourite leather jacket, the one she wore every day in spite of the weather. Cassie rubbed her fingers over its soft leather and across the smooth red satin of its interior lining.

Of course. Faye had sewn the garter into the jacket's lining. It made perfect sense.

Cassie clawed at the red satin until she broke through its surface and tore it wide open. And there it was, resting in a bed of supple red satin – the green leather garter. Cassie was about to reach into the material to pluck it free when she remembered the sparks that burned her fingers earlier. She retrieved the obsidian crystal from her pocket once more and glided it over and around the garter to disable any spell Faye had on it. Then she was free to reach out and grab it. At last.

The garter felt heavy and triumphant in her hand. She gripped it tightly, admiring its shiny buckles, hardly believing she'd done it. She'd really done it! But there was no time to celebrate. Cassie could hear the orange cat scratching outside Faye's bedroom door, and she had to escape before Faye woke up again.

Soundlessly, she tried to patch the lining back into place, but without a needle and thread or the proper spell, it would be impossible. Faye would discover it missing in the morning – that was unavoidable. But it didn't matter.

Cassie would be in Cape Cod by then, with the power of all the Master Tools along with her.

She left the jacket hanging like a looted grave, slipped out of the closet, and across the bedroom floor. The moment she opened the door, the orange cat leaped in, but Cassie was down the stairs and out the way she came within seconds.

It was only then, finally, that she let the reality settle over her. She now possessed all of the Master Tools, and the power she needed to save Scarlett, even without the help of the Circle.

Chapter Twenty-Six

Cassie woke up at five the next morning, on the dot, without her alarm. It was like her body was so attuned to the day's mission that man-made technologies of convenience, like clocks, were deemed unnecessary. She felt one with the elements today, no longer at their mercy.

She got up from bed and dressed ceremonially, like a Spartan warrior preparing for battle. She wrapped herself in the white shift Diana had given her and proudly snapped the silver cuff-bracelet onto her upper arm, the leather garter around her thigh and the sparkling diadem upon her head. She was ready to go save her sister.

Cassie made her way downstairs to the kitchen. She had to borrow her mother's car, but she couldn't exactly tell her mother she needed it so she could battle the witch

The Divide

hunters and save the sister she was never told about. So she'd have to take it without asking. That seemed to be the theme of this entire mission: take what you need to get the job done and explain later. And she would. All would be revealed later, to her mother, to Diana, Faye, Adam, everyone. For now, Cassie couldn't allow any guilt to creep up and distract her – she had to focus solely on getting to Cape Cod.

But as Cassie drove farther away from Crowhaven Road and then farther away from New Salem, a sickness inside her began to form. Nerves, she figured, and she told herself she had every right to feel nervous; this was a dangerous act. The hunters had black magic on their side.

The Master Tools will not let me down in my moment of need, Cassie thought. And that reminded her of the chalcedony rose she had hidden within her pocket.

It was the good-luck piece Adam gave her long ago in case she was in trouble – she'd brought it with her just in case. After everything they'd been through and disagreed over these past few weeks, Cassie still believed in Adam and had faith in their bond. Did they need a rare crystal to connect them at this point in their relationship? No, of course not. Maybe Cassie only brought the chalcedony

249

piece out of superstition, but even so, it calmed her to stroke its rugged surface. The stone felt alive in her grasp the way it did when Adam had first given it to her. *Hold on to it tight*, he'd told her, *and think of me*. She did that now and felt her courage grow.

But crossing over the county line into the town of Sandwich, Cassie's fear heightened to a new level. The decaying sign alerting that she'd arrived read: INCORPORATED 1639, reminding Cassie of the deep-rooted history of the place as the oldest town in Cape Cod. The Tools themselves seemed to react to the setting all on their own. Cassie could swear they were warming to her body, growing hotter by the second as she followed the course she'd mapped out to Hawthorne Street.

She should have a plan of attack, she realised, for when she encountered the hunters. She knew the witch-hunter curse by heart, and the Tools would surely come to her aid, but now that the reality of the situation was setting in, questions began to form in Cassie's mind. She didn't know how many hunters there would be. Was there a limit to how many she could take down with the one curse? And what if Scarlett was in even worse shape when she arrived than in Cassie's dream? There was a fear lurking in the back of Cassie's mind that Scarlett could have already been killed.

Again, Cassie felt for the chalcedony rose. But even with the crystal's comfort, when the house at 48 Hawthorne Street came into view, her whole being flooded with fear. It was just as she'd imagined it in her nightmares, identical to the image that came to her during the location spell. It was a broken-down beach cottage with driftwood-grey siding, and it was near the end of a long, desolate, sandy lane, with a large body of water on one side and tidal marshes on the other. There was no other house in sight.

The terrible feeling in Cassie's gut grew. The acid from her stomach crept up her throat, filling her mouth with a sickening taste. Every inch of her body screamed for her to turn around and drive back home. But she knew she couldn't allow her fear to get the best of her now. Not when she'd come this far.

With determination, she got out of the car and trod across the long grass towards the house, but after only a few steps she froze. She tried to continue forward and couldn't. There was some kind of magical barrier protecting the house's perimeter, similar to the one Faye used to guard the hidden garter. But that would be easy enough for Cassie to penetrate while wearing the Tools.

She touched each relic individually, adjusting them into place, and silently called on their collective power. It wasn't her imagination; the Tools did feel hot to her touch, she was sure of it.

'Be now dissolved, powerful shield!' Her voice left her throat sounding deep and gravelly as she sent all of her energy towards the house. She focused hard and said the words again, this time pushing with her mind until she felt the power of the Tools rush out of her like a blistering heat.

The spell seemed to work at once. The dark cloud perched over the house cleared, and the guarding force at the property's perimeter disappeared. *The relics are really working*, Cassie thought to herself. Scarlett was as good as saved.

Without delay, she continued forward unhindered. Practising the witch-hunter curse in her mind, she walked slowly and carefully in a state of deep meditation towards the house.

When she was inches away from the front door, she could see it was windblown and water-damaged, rotted to a softness no wood should be. And the foundation of the house creaked and rattled in the wind, like it could come crashing down at any moment. It occurred to Cassie to try some kind of protection spell on herself before entering, or maybe another silence spell to assist her in sneaking into the house. But then she thought better of it. She would step inside just as she was, no cowardly tricks, no sleight of hand. The Tools were the only power she needed.

Cassie listened for voices but heard none. In the eerie silence, the fear that Scarlett had already been killed raced through her mind. An image of her dead body hanging from the ceiling, swinging back and forth, like the arm of a clock – *tick tock, tick tock* – haunted Cassie. But she couldn't step through this door with the slightest bit of distraction. She'd have seconds to cast the curse, less than that in fact. Cast the curse, rescue Scarlett, and then get the heck out of there. That was the plan.

Carefully, Cassie placed her hand upon the rotted softness of the door. To her surprise, it wasn't locked. In fact, it didn't even appear to be fully closed. She pushed on its damp surface gently with the palm of her hand, and it swept open effortlessly. She was already chanting the witch-hunter curse under her breath, ready for anything that came at her, but when she stepped inside, the scene was nothing like what she saw in her dreams.

The main room was large and tidy. Its walls were

painted an oceanic blue and were finished with bright white crown moulding. The hardwood floors were freshly waxed and the air inside the room was warm and cedarscented with the heat of a wood-burning fire.

Scarlett was there, by herself, lounging on a faded sofa in front of the fireplace. Her dyed-red hair cascaded in healthy waves onto her shoulders, framing her rosy-cheeked smirking face.

'Finally,' she said. 'I've been getting so bored up here waiting for you.'

Instantly Cassie knew she'd made a terrible mistake. This was all a trap.

Chapter Twenty-Seven

'Come have a seat by the fire,' Scarlett said. She was smiling, in a twisted kind of way.

Cassie tried to run back out the door, but she found her feet planted in place once again, just as they had been outside on the perimeter of the property. 'What's going on?' she asked.

'You can come in closer, you just can't leave.' Scarlett's smile brightened.

'Where are the hunters?' Cassie asked.

Scarlett shrugged her shoulders. 'Don't know.'

'Are they even real?'

'Oh, the hunters are very real,' Scarlett said. 'They killed my mother and they followed me here. They just never caught me.'

She tapped the empty space on the sofa beside her,

indicating Cassie to sit. 'Your Circle has no idea what they're in for with the hunters. But they offered the perfect set-up while I practised my mind-invasion spells.'

So all this time Cassie thought she was having visions, communicating across space and time to her sister, it was all just a trick. The Circle had been right all along. Cassie hadn't been thinking clearly.

Cassie couldn't turn around and run away, but she still had the Tools and they were quivering with energy. She could protect herself.

She touched each relic and called on their power. Immediately, the Tools became hot – this time, too hot. They singed her skin like they'd turned against her.

'Feel the burn?' Scarlett asked.

She had somehow gotten the Tools to backfire on Cassie. They became angry and restless, sizzling with torment.

'I'll take them off your hands,' Scarlett said.

Effortlessly, with one snap of her finger, the Master Tools obeyed her call. Like metal to a magnet, they unhinged themselves from Cassie's body and flew at Scarlett's outstretched hands.

But how? How did Scarlett have so much influence over the Tools that she could beckon them? She must have been a more powerful witch than Cassie could have ever imagined.

'It really is a shame you've never dabbled in the dark arts,' Scarlett said, sensing Cassie's amazement at her abilities.

Suddenly Cassie felt cold and naked, wearing nothing but the white shift. Powerless and bewildered, she shivered.

'Who are you?' she asked.

'I'm Black John's daughter. Isn't that obvious?' Scarlett said, gesturing at the Master Tools.

'So we really are sisters.'

'Oh yeah,' Scarlett said. 'That part was real.'

Scarlett, now wearing the Master Tools over her black T-shirt and jeans, reached for a poker from the fireplace. Cassie stiffened, but then relaxed when Scarlett leaned over the side of the couch to an open bag of marshmallows. She skewered one with the black metal poker and held it over the fire.

'These Tools were meant for me,' Scarlett said. 'Your whole life was meant for me.'

'I don't believe you,' Cassie said, trying her best to come off sounding strong and controlled. 'I have no reason to believe anything you say.'

Scarlett laughed. 'You have every reason to.' She watched the marshmallow reluctantly brown over the flame. She seemed to enjoy the way it struggled to maintain its exterior before succumbing to the heat.

'I was the one he intended to be in the Circle with the rest of them,' she said. 'I was born in November, like the others. Not you. Everything you've enjoyed since you arrived in New Salem – all of it rightfully belongs to me.'

'No,' Cassie said. It couldn't be true.

'Yup. You were just an afterthought, a back-up plan.'

Cassie felt sick. And the sugary scent of burning marshmallow wasn't helping.

Scarlett rotated the poker in her hand like a rotisserie. 'And now I'm here to claim my rightful spot in the Circle. But I'm going to have to kill you to get it.'

She turned her shining black eyes onto Cassie. 'Isn't that a bummer, sis?'

Scarlett gripped the metal poker with both hands and Cassie realised just how much danger she was in. Scarlett did seem just crazy enough to kill her. She had to try to talk her way out of this.

'Why kill me,' Cassie asked, 'when we could lead the Circle together?'

Scarlett widened her eyes. 'Really?' Her voice came

out sounding childlike. 'You'd be willing to do that?'

Cassie nodded energetically. 'Of course,' she said, trying to sound believable. 'We'll kick someone else out to make room for you as the twelfth member. Trust me, there are plenty of weak links.'

Scarlett's dark-red lips curled into a vicious smile, and she laughed with her whole body. 'You really are pathetic,' she said. 'You don't know much, but even you know it doesn't work that way.'

She pulled the poker out of the flames. The burned marshmallow on its tip was now on fire, burning red like a hot coal.

'Someone has to die to break the Circle's bond,' Scarlett said. 'And whichever member dies, they're immediately replaced with someone of their own bloodline.'

She shoved the flaming tip of the pointer under Cassie's nose. 'Didn't you know that? Or had you and your little friends not gotten to that lesson in witch school?

'You made for mostly an easy target,' Scarlett continued. 'Until that protection spell made it impossible to kill you in New Salem.'

'You were the one who cut my brakes,' Cassie said. It had finally all began making sense.

Scarlett ignored the accusation. 'But now you're

vulnerable,' she said. 'No protection spell. And without even your precious Circle to save you.'

Cassie tried to think of a spell, any spell, to help her out of this situation, but none came to mind. It was like her brain had reset to a blank page. Scarlett had somehow rendered her completely powerless.

'And since you brought the Master Tools right to me, killing you should be easy.' Scarlett urged the fireball-tipped poker an inch away from Cassie's face.

She's going to burn me, Cassie thought. *She's going to set me on fire.*

'Don't waste your energy trying to do a spell,' Scarlett said. 'Only black magic works in this house.'

Black magic. That explained it, all of it.

Cassie may have lacked the words to call on the element of Water, but she had to do something. With no other options, she took a swing at the poker, knowing full well she'd burn her hand doing so, but it worked. She knocked the weapon from Scarlett's grasp across the room. It landed with a thump onto the thick throw rug.

Cassie was mildly proud of herself, but Scarlett didn't seem the least bit rattled that she'd deflected the burning poker from her grasp.

'Nice work,' Scarlett said. 'I couldn't have done that

better myself.' She directed Cassie's attention to the smoke rising up from the rug where the poker had landed. Then the smoke gave way to a small, newly born flame.

Scarlett's dark eyes sparkled, reflecting the silver of the diadem and bracelet, and the buckles of the garter. With a single wave of her hand, she fanned the small fire across the entire floor and up all four walls of the cottage, surrounding Cassie in a sweltering tent of heat and flames.

I'm a fool, Cassie thought, *a fool for being so trusting*.

Cassie cowered at the sight of the fire. There was no escaping a blaze of this size.

'You've gone too far,' Cassie cried out. 'You'll burn in here with me.'

Scarlett stood up and calmly began walking through the flames to gather her things. 'Another thing you don't know,' she said, yanking her clothes out of the closet and stuffing them into a large duffel bag. 'The fire protection spell. It was one of Daddy's favourites.'

Smoke filled the room. It caught Cassie in the throat and brought stinging tears to her eyes, but Scarlett remained unbothered by it.

'No!' Cassie screamed, crawling across the floor towards Scarlett, but she could only move a few inches in any direction. The flames were blocking her every exit. Within minutes the fire would consume her. 'Please, Scarlett, we're sisters. Please don't do this!'

Scarlett stood still with her bags in hand. Angry flames danced and cracked all around her, and black smoke encircled her body like a sinister tornado. 'At least go with a little dignity, Cassie.'

She dropped her bags in place and took a few deliberate steps closer. She leaned down slowly, like a serpent, to look Cassie in the eyes. 'Did our father scream for mercy when you killed him, Cassie? I bet not.'

Scarlett had *his* eyes, Cassie realised. Those pitch-black marbles that were cold as death, just like Black John's. She was more his daughter than Cassie was. How could Cassie have been so fooled by her before?

And then Cassie remembered her mother's words about Black John. *He wasn't all bad*, she'd said.

'You don't have to do this,' Cassie cried, trying to soften Scarlett's cold hard stare with her own. 'There's good inside you, even now. You can choose to not be like him.'

'I know.' Scarlett kicked Cassie away with the heel of her black boot. 'But where's the fun in that?'

Chapter Twenty-Eight

The flames roared and crackled with evil intent, as if the fire had a will of its own. Its scorching heat brought Cassie, blistering, to her knees. She was coughing and couldn't catch her breath, soon to completely lose herself to its all-consuming power. Scarlett looked her over one last time.

'Goodbye, Cassie,' she said. 'It was nice knowing you.'

Cassie's face burned from the sweltering heat. This must be what hell would feel like, she thought, this never-ending torture by fire. Cut off from her mother, and her friends, and Adam, Cassie was dying alone. And here was Scarlett, the stronger daughter, the wicked sister, and the last living face Cassie would look upon before her death.

But she couldn't give up. She forced herself to her feet

and got as close to Scarlett as the flames would allow. The Tools had darkened to a sinister sheen on Scarlett's body. *Black John is in her*, Cassie thought.

But he is also in me.

Scarlett seemed to notice a change in Cassie's eyes. It was enough to cause her to back away.

'He is in me,' Cassie said, aloud this time, and it powered up some secret recess within her, like an emergency generator that kicks on in a blackout.

Scarlett continued backing away, through the flames, towards the exit. The fire protection spell was still working for her, but she was suddenly afraid.

The power of fire, Cassie thought. *The power of fire is in me.*

And then something cracked open somewhere deep inside Cassie's chest, that dark space she'd never accessed before. It frightened her, the burst of energy she felt as the word left her lips. 'Burn!' she commanded.

And Scarlett did. Midway through the flames on her way to the door, she screamed as brutally as Cassie had heard in her nightmare. No longer was she protected from the fire, no longer could she step safely from the burning house to the cool air outside.

Scarlett jumped back from the door, furiously batting

out the flames from her clothes. Then she turned to Cassie. 'I thought you were good,' she said.

Cassie stood tall, newly energised. 'Likewise.'

Cassie could feel something churning deep within her gut. It rose up her throat like black bile and escaped her mouth as a scream that caused the kitchen tap to rupture into a geyser. Then the walls shook and every pipe within them burst, spurting cold water across the room in diagonal torrents. The fire was extinguished within seconds.

Scarlett drew away, shocked by this turn of events, but she had her own commands at her disposal as well as the Master Tools to enhance her power. '*Fragilis!*' she shouted, thrusting her open palms at Cassie.

It was a Latin spell Cassie didn't understand, but it made her drop to the floor like all the energy had been drained out of her. Her body felt heavy and the room began to spin. She couldn't even lift her head.

'*Sentis infirma.*' Scarlett directed her charged fingers to Cassie's head and then her heart.

Cassie became so feeble and tired, woozy to the point of faintness, she was sure she was dying.

This is it, Cassie thought. *Scarlett is just too strong.* She'd lost.

She wished that she could see Adam at that moment, to have his be the last face she looked upon before going to her death. She remembered the chalcedony rose in her pocket and limply felt for it. It took all the energy she had left to work it into her hand. She squeezed it as tightly as her fingers would allow and imagined Adam's strong, loving face with such concentration that she swore he actually appeared. The smoke cleared, and Adam's dark-red hair seemed to her so close and real, she believed she could see its every highlight. This must be what dying was. Cassie was too weak to smile, but she was grateful her final wish had come true.

It took a second for Cassie to realise that Adam was actually in the house standing over her. It really was him. He took her face into his hands and called out her name. She felt herself falling in and out of consciousness. Like in her nightmares and visions, her sight was both cloudy and vivid at the same time, a disordered, mystifying confusion. But the connection between her and Adam in this heightened moment was intense. The silver cord that hummed between them materialised, brighter and more pronounced than Cassie had ever seen it before. It appeared so lifelike, she swore she could reach out and touch it with her fingertips. Her chest overfilled with love as she followed the cord's path from Adam's heart to her own. But then as she looked closer, she noticed something strange. There were two silver cords. One was reaching from Adam to her and the other was reaching from Adam to Scarlett.

In a flash, both cords were gone. Just like that. Cassie wasn't even sure Adam saw it.

That had to be a mistake, a hallucination. It was impossible to decipher what was real any more and what was her imagination.

'Cassie.' Adam still had her face in his hands. 'Stay with me, Cassie. Stay awake.'

She blinked away the tears that filled her eyes and turned to see all of them there – Diana and the rest of the Circle. They had Scarlett surrounded.

'Give us the Master Tools,' Diana said. 'And we won't have to hurt you.'

'I'd like to see you try.' Scarlett laughed.

Diana stood motionless. It took a moment for her to realise she couldn't do magic, but once she did, Scarlett hurled her hands at her. *'Praestrangulo,'* she said.

Instantly Diana clutched her throat with both hands and dropped to her knees, struggling to breathe.

'She's suffocating!' Adam jumped to his feet, and Cassie

cried out, but she was still too weak stop him. He charged towards Scarlett, chanting, 'Earth my body, water my blood.'

Faye and the others fell in behind him. 'Earth my body, water my blood, air my breath and fire my spirit!'

Cassie screamed, 'It won't work!' But none of them would listen, or maybe her screaming was only as loud as a whisper. She couldn't tell.

'*Caecitas!*' Scarlett fanned her hand at the group.

Adam cried out first. 'I can't see,' he said. And then, one by one, each of them shrieked, covering their eyes. Scarlett had blinded them.

Diana was writhing on the floor, turning blue and coughing. Cassie had no strength, but she had to do something. The darkness was in her; she couldn't be afraid to reach down into it. Even if it killed her, it was the only way to save her friends.

It took all her might to climb to her feet.

Scarlett, seeing her get up, grabbed her bags and ran for the door.

Cassie pushed with her mind and let loose a debilitating cry. 'Scarlett!'

She searched her soul for the words, the darkest most

debilitating spell she could think of, but Scarlett was out the door and gone within seconds.

'Magicae negrae conversam,' Cassie said feebly. Those were the words that came to her after Scarlett had escaped.

Diana gasped and inhaled. Adam blinked his eyes back to sight. Slowly, everyone regained their senses. Cassie's strength returned, and she went to Adam and held him. There were scratches where he'd been clawing at his eyelids.

'Did you just undo Scarlett's spells?' he asked.

Cassie nodded, and then she looked at the sooty, sweaty faces of her friends who'd risked their lives to save her. How could she ever apologise enough for what they'd just been through?

'I was wrong about Scarlett,' she said. 'But I guess you figured that out by now.'

The tint of suffocation still hadn't fully left Diana's face. 'What just happened?' she asked. 'Scarlett was untouchable.'

'You were right that she's evil,' Cassie said, hardly able to look Diana in the eye. 'She was doing black magic. She said that was the only magic that would work here. That's why none of you could cast spells.'

'But then how did you—' Diana stopped herself mid-question, when the answer occurred to her.

Cassie looked down. She could hear Faye walk a circle around the burned-out room, her boots crackling upon the ruined floor with each step.

'I knew it all along,' Faye said. 'Cassie has black magic in her.'

It was true. There was no use denying it, as much as Cassie wanted to.

Cassie searched Adam's face for a reaction, terrified of what it might be.

But Adam's eyes filled with tears and he pulled Cassie in towards his chest. 'I'm so glad you're okay,' he said.

Cassie didn't feel like she deserved his comforting, and tried to break free from his arms.

Adam squeezed her tighter. 'You just saved our lives,' he said.

'I almost cost you your lives,' Cassie said, no longer able to stop herself from crying. 'All of this is my fault. All of it, and I am so sorry.'

Diana placed her hand on Cassie's back. 'We're all in this together,' she said. 'And we're all okay. That's what matters.'

Cassie began to sob into Adam's chest. 'But I want to be good.'

'You are good.' Diana hugged Cassie from behind, sandwiching her between herself and Adam. 'You can't start doubting that.'

'Scarlett is the evil one,' Adam said. 'Not you.'

Cassie appreciated their support. They meant well, and she knew that, but the truth was, none of them could be sure what the ability to perform black magic meant for Cassie.

Faye smiled at her like a new discovery. 'How does it feel?' she asked.

'I just feel like going home,' Cassie said.

Chapter Twenty-Nine

They all recovered from the morning's battle miraculously well. A little soap and water, and a change of clothes, and each of them were mostly back to their old selves.

Diana prepared a herbal tea in the kitchen and returned to the living room carrying a tray. 'Is Faye here yet?' she asked.

The Circle was desperate to hear what had happened at Cape Cod before they arrived and to fill in the holes of what they still didn't understand.

'We should start without her,' Suzan said, picking at her nail cuticles.

Diana shot Adam a concerned look and asked Suzan, 'Where is she?'

'We know exactly where she is,' Laurel said. 'She's with Max.'

'I didn't tell you that,' Suzan said.

'Maybe we should begin without her,' Cassie said. She knew how unbelievably lucky it was that none of them had been badly hurt and she was anxious to apologise again for her mistakes. 'I want to make sure I don't ever put any of you at risk again. So I have a lot to tell you.'

Just then Faye swept through the door. Her eyes were infused with an energy that was palpable. Her cheeks were flushed, and her plump red lips looked almost like they were swollen with blood.

'Sorry I'm late,' she said.

'You need to quit it with Max already,' Adam said. 'How many times do we have to tell you? We don't know if we can trust him.'

Faye felt for a black pendant hanging from her neck, and Cassie caught something unusual in her eyes.

'I said I was sorry.' Faye continued toying with the pendant. She always wore a red star ruby necklace, but the pendant was new. It was a shimmering black opal.

'Did Max give you that?' Cassie asked.

Faye let go of the necklace immediately and shot Cassie a threatening look, but Cassie noticed that she also blushed. All at once, Cassie realised the truth: Faye's feelings for Max were real.

Melanie exhaled loudly. 'Don't we have more important things to talk about than Faye's love life?'

'Yes, we do,' Diana said. 'Cassie, why don't you fill us in on what we missed?'

Cassie stepped to the centre of the room. 'First, I want to apologise formally to all of you,' she said. 'I should have never betrayed you the way I did. Especially my fellow leaders, Diana and Faye.'

'An apology isn't necessary,' Nick said from where he was sitting in the corner.

There were nods all around.

Faye scoffed. 'I can't believe you pansies are letting her off this easy. If it were me who'd stolen the Master Tools, and then lost them to boot—'

'The Circle forgives you, Cassie,' Diana said, cutting Faye off. 'But remember, for the future, that we're your family, too.'

'I know that now,' Cassie said. 'I knew it before, but I guess it slipped away from me.'

Cassie's heart was thumping in her chest. 'You've been a sister to me since I arrived here,' she said to Diana. 'And you're the only sister I'll ever need.'

Diana's eyes misted over. 'Thank you,' she said.

Melanie cleared her throat. 'I hate to interrupt this

274

sentimental moment, but maybe Cassie can tell us what she learned about Scarlett, so we know what we're up against.'

'Of course,' Cassie said. She went on to explain how Scarlett had tricked her, to lure her away from the protective spell, and that Scarlett was the daughter Black John intended for the Circle.

Nick walked solemnly over to Cassie. 'So Scarlett wants to kill you.'

'Yes,' Cassie said. 'So she can have my place in the Circle, because we're the same bloodline.'

'What about the witch hunters?' Melanie asked. 'Who killed Great-Aunt Constance and Portia?'

'And who burned the symbol onto my front lawn?' Laurel asked, her voice high-pitched with fright.

Cassie took a deep breath. 'The hunters are real and they're still out there. But Scarlett had nothing to do with them. She just seized the opportunity to use our fear of the hunters against us.'

'We are so screwed,' Faye said, and Cassie noticed her reach for the pendant again. There was something about it drawing Cassie in, the way it caught the light.

'Can I get a closer look at that?' she asked, reaching for it. Before Faye could resist, Cassie caught the stone in her hand and studied its surface. It was slightly translucent, not totally black, but a play of green and blue and red. As Cassie tilted it back and forth, she noticed how it diffracted the light in a continually changing play of colour.

The moment Cassie saw it, her blood ran cold. Camouflaged within the opal's fascinating surface was the hunter symbol, shimmering iridescently.

'Oh my God,' Cassie said. 'Faye, you've been marked.'

The rest of the group gasped.

'That's not possible,' Faye said. She looked down at the necklace. 'No!' she screamed, recognising the symbol immediately. 'He couldn't have!'

For a few minutes, nobody spoke. Cassie glanced around the room at each of her friends. How quickly the energy of the room had shifted. The almighty Faye had fallen.

Faye looked like a different person. Her broad shoulders were rounded forward and all the colour had drained from her face. She sat down on the couch, slumped over crying. It was a sight none of them could fathom.

'How?' she asked. Her eyes were bloodshot, and black mascara streamed down her face. It was the first time Cassie had ever seen Faye cry. 'I just don't understand how this could have happened.'

'Max is a witch hunter,' Melanie declared. 'He's the one who gave that to you.'

'And that means the principal is probably a hunter, too.' Adam glanced at Cassie with meaning. 'Just like you suspected.'

Melanie nodded. 'Like father, like son.'

Cassie couldn't feel good about being right about the principal, especially at a moment like this. She would rather it had turned out to be silly paranoia.

Diana sat down beside Faye and gently took her hand. 'I know you're still in shock, Faye, but we need to know everything you've told Max.'

Faye lifted her head. Tears hung from her dark lashes, and her expression was beyond stricken. 'I don't even remember.'

She unclasped the necklace from behind her neck and dropped it onto the table. 'I thought he really liked me,' she said softly, almost to herself. 'I didn't want to tell you all this, but I undid the love spell a while ago. To see if his feelings were . . .' She couldn't even say it.

Diana wrapped both her arms around Faye and, unbelievably, she let her. Cassie had to look away. Seeing Faye heartbroken was nearly as brutal as seeing her marked.

'But he seemed so overpowered by the spell,' Laurel said.

'He might have been resistant to her magic the whole time, but was playing along to get close to us,' Adam said.

Cassie shot Adam a look to quiet him. He and Laurel may have been putting the necessary pieces together, but they could do it in the other room, where Faye wouldn't hear them. They were unaware of the effect their words were having on her as she began crying harder. But Cassie understood. When Faye undid the love spell and Max was still acting like he couldn't live without her, she mistook it for true love.

Melanie shook her head in disbelief. 'So the hunters know about two of us,' she said. 'And without the Master Tools, we're not strong enough to fight them.'

'And Scarlett still wants to kill Cassie,' Nick said.

Diana continued holding Faye in her arms. 'There's no time to panic,' she said, but her voice was trembling. 'It's time to come together to support and protect one another.'

She focused her eyes directly on Cassie. 'We'll figure out a way,' she said. 'We always do.'

Chapter Thirty

From her front porch, Cassie could see the flickering blue of the television flashing like a strobe light in a haunted house. Her mother must be waiting up for her.

'I should go right in,' Cassie said, gripping the door handle. 'She's up.'

'Not yet.' Adam reached for her hand and squeezed it. 'With everything going on,' he said, 'and everything that's happened, I want you to know that we'll get through it.'

'I know,' Cassie said.

'Are you sure?' He leaned in for a kiss, but he stopped just shy of her lips.

Cassie could feel his breath on her skin and the warmth of his body so close to hers. She held his gaze and her heart pounded heavily in her chest.

'I'm positive.' She pulled him in towards her, meeting

his soft lips with hers. With a wild abandon she had forgotten, she and Adam melded into one, and she let herself be swept away.

They kissed like that until they were both heated and flushed. Cassie allowed her breathing to slow and her heart to settle. Then she stared up at him, captivated for a moment by the course of life pulsing between them. The silver cord, she thought, the mystifying bond that had connected her to him from the beginning, and always would. It was stronger now than ever. After the wild mix of emotions Cassie had experienced these past few weeks, one thing emerged solid and bright. She realised in a whole new way just how lucky she was to have Adam by her side.

'I love you,' she said.

He smiled brightly. 'And I love you.'

She kissed him once more, tenderly, and inhaled a full breath of him. 'I really love you,' she said.

His blue eyes sparkled and he laughed aloud. 'We can play this game all night.'

'Or our whole lives,' Cassie said, beaming back at him. She found she couldn't take her eyes from his. They drew her closer and closer in.

'Maybe even longer.'

* * *

When Cassie finally made her way into the house, she shut the front door behind her and paused. Her mother looked almost like a ghost and about as frightened as if she'd seen one. Cassie felt awful she'd caused her to worry so much. Her mother had every right to be angry with her.

'Mom,' she said, 'I am so sorry.'

When her mother made no response, she added, 'I needed to go to Cape Cod; it was an emergency. And then—'

'Forget about the car,' her mother said. 'Are you okay?'

Cassie nodded and dropped her bag at the door. When she reached her mother's arms, she looked up at her, hoping to see a sign of reprieve in her eyes. But instead, a saddened expression passed over her mother's face, like a massive wave of pain.

'Mom?' Cassie asked, not even sure what to say.

Her mother's large black eyes, shadowed by dark circles, filled with tears. 'I thought you ran away,' she said. 'And then I thought you were dead. I swear I could feel your pain.'

She spoke quietly and regretfully, and Cassie realised

her mother probably could feel when she was in pain. They were connected, and she was a witch, after all.

'You seem to be pulling away from me, just when I thought we were becoming closer,' her mother said. 'Was it something I did or said that upset you? Tell me.'

When Cassie found out her mother kept Scarlett a secret, it seemed like such a betrayal, like the worst secret in the world to keep hidden for her entire life. But now, looking at her mother's frail, penitent face, Cassie realised she'd done it to protect her. She must have known Scarlett was evil.

'Oh, Mom,' Cassie said. 'I wasn't angry, just confused. I was confused about so much.'

After everything that had happened, Cassie realised it was time to finally tell her mom the truth.

'I have so much to tell you,' Cassie said.

Cassie didn't even know where to begin, but she did her best to speak evenly and not leave anything out. She dug her nails into her palms and went on, uninterrupted, for what felt like forever. Then her mother took a shallow breath in and shut her eyes. Cassie knew it was time to be quiet and let her speak.

'Scarlett's mother didn't shy away from the dark side of Black John either,' she said. 'She'd been banned from our Circle for performing dark magic. But I'd hoped those days were behind us now. That's why I never mentioned Scarlett.'

Cassie nodded, and her mother took her face into her hands. 'I would have never kept it from you if I thought you were in danger.'

'It's not your fault,' Cassie said. 'I should have told you when I found out about her.'

'It's not anybody's fault,' her mother said. 'But it's still come to this.' She took a deep breath and stood up.

'There's something I've been waiting to give you until it was necessary,' she said cryptically. 'Now seems to be that time.'

The tone of her voice was puzzling. 'What is it?' Cassie asked.

'I'll be right back.'

Her mother left the room and was gone longer than Cassie expected her to be. But just when Cassie was about to go looking for her, she returned with a book in her hands. It was a faded leather-bound journal with gold, deckle-edged pages. It looked to Cassie like an old Bible.

'This was your father's Book of Shadows,' her mother said, holding it out to her with both hands.

Cassie froze, paralysed, and felt the blood drain out of

her face. Black John's Book of Shadows – just the thought of it made her shudder. Black magic was something she felt was better left unexplored.

Her mother continued holding the book out to her. 'It's okay,' she said. 'You can touch it.'

Cassie reached out to take it from her mother reluctantly. The book felt cruel and cold in her hands – it almost felt alive.

'How did you get this?' Cassie asked.

Her mother sat back down beside her. 'It's a long story. But it's been hidden here in this house for quite some time. You have to understand, in the wrong hands this book could be extremely dangerous.'

Like the Master Tools, Cassie thought. 'And you want me to have it?'

Her mother's face was stern. 'You'll need it if you stand any chance of defeating Scarlett.'

The book was heavier than it appeared to be, like its contents were greater than the sum of its pages. It was impossible to comprehend the dark spells and secrets it enclosed. Cassie noticed that its black leather cover wasn't completely smooth. It was faintly embossed with a symbol that reminded Cassie of the inscriptions on the silver bracelet and the diadem. There were also dull scratches and indentations, like fingernails had worn into its surface. And its upper-right-hand corner was eroded almost completely grey, like a deteriorated oval-shaped stamp.

Black John's fingerprint, Cassie realised.

She jerked her eyes away from the greyed spot and her stomach lurched. She was intrigued by it, but it also upset her.

Cassie refocused on the embossed symbol, trying to remember where else she'd seen that design. And then she remembered: it was identical to the inscription on Black John's lodestone ring, the one used to identify him as John Blake, and later as John Brunswick.

Having this book in her hands was the closest thing now to having Black John there in the room with her. It felt like all the darkness in the world might begin to pour forth from its pages at any moment.

Cassie's mother watched her handle the book apprehensively. 'I know it feels alive to you,' she said. 'But it's just a book, I promise. And you are strong enough to handle it.' There was a candidness in her eyes that Cassie had never seen before.

The book shivered in Cassie's hands as she tried to calm herself. It was just paper and words, that's all it was.

And its words contained the key to defeating Scarlett, saving the Circle and getting the Master Tools back. She didn't have the luxury of pretending this book didn't exist, as evil and frightening as it felt to her. She couldn't simply put it back into its hiding place. It was her responsibility to read it, study it and ingest its secrets until they became part of who she was. Only then would she be strong enough against Scarlett.

Her mother silently observed her mental struggle and seemed to know exactly what she was thinking.

'Remember, Cassie,' she said. 'There's so much goodness in you. There's much more light in your soul than dark. Do you recognise that?'

Cassie nodded. 'I think so.'

'But there are things in this book that won't be easy for you to read. Do you understand what I mean by that?'

'Yes,' Cassie said.

'If you open it,' her mother warned, 'there's no going back.'

THE SECRET CIRCLE

THE INITIATION AND THE CAPTIVE PART I

Cassie is not happy about moving from sunny California to gloomy New England. She longs for her old life, her old friends … But when she starts to form a bond with a clique of terrifying but seductive teenagers at her new school, she thinks maybe she could fit in after all …

Initiated into the Secret Circle, she is pulled along by the deadly and intoxicating thrill of this powerful and gifted coven. But then she falls in love, and has a daunting choice to make. She must resist temptation or risk dark forces to get what she wants.

THE SECRET CIRCLE

THE CAPTIVE PART II AND THE POWER

Now that Cassie is part of the most alluring and deadly clique imaginable, she is starting to realise that power comes with a price – more dangerous than she knows. Torn between the opposing desires of the two leaders of the Secret Circle, Cassie is struggling again. Does she use her considerable supernatural power to save lives, or does she put all her energy into keeping Adam, the boy she loves.

Cassie's relationship with Adam is threatening to tear the circle apart, so where does Cassie's loyalty and strength, truly lie?

Vampire Diaries

November 2012

the Vampire Diaries

Stefan's Diaries

Stefan and Damon weren't always fighting or succumbing to their bloodlusts. Once they were loving siblings who enjoyed all the riches and happiness that their wealthy lifestyle afforded them; loyal brothers who happened to both fall for the same beautiful woman. Once they were alive...

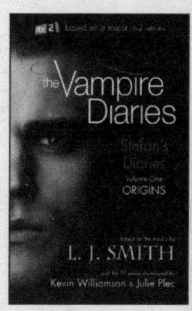

NIGHT WORLD

Welcome to the Night World -
a secret world of vampires, werewolves,
witches, shapeshifters, and ancient souls
where humans are prey and relationships
with them forbidden. But we all know,
there's nothing like forbidden fruit ...

placeholder